"You look a little tired," Dan said. "So let's call it a morning. We can meet back here this afternoon."

"But Dan," Tori complained, "I still haven't gotten all the way through my short program." Tori's muscles were aching, but she didn't want to stop. At least ten of the other skaters she'd be competing against were still on the ice, working hard.

"Tor, you look tired. You're not focusing," Dan said. "Trust me, it's time to call it a morning."

Tori frowned, but she knew better than to argue with Dan. He was easygoing, but he was also stubborn. She stepped off the ice. Dan handed over her skate guards, and Tori slipped them on.

Nothing is going right today, she thought. *Nothing.* She turned around and looked back at the ice. Jill was on the opposite end of the rink, holding her leg high in a graceful spiral. Amber was launching into a triple salchow. The young girl landed the jump flawlessly.

I don't stand a chance, Tori thought miserably. I never should have come here!

Gold Medal Dreams #2

NOW OR NEVER

Melissa Lowell

Created by Parachute Press, Inc.

A SKYLARK BOOK
NEW YORK • TORONTO • LONDON • SYDNEY • AUCKLAND

With special thanks to Darlene Parent, director of
Sky Rink Skating School, New York City,
and the choreographer of Tori's skating routines.

RL 5.2, 009–012

NOW OR NEVER

A Skylark Book / January 1998

Skylark Books is a registered trademark of Bantam Books,
a division of Bantam Doubleday Dell Publishing Group, Inc.
Registered in U.S. Patent and Trademark Office and elsewhere.

Silver Blades® is a registered trademark of Parachute Press, Inc.
The logos of the United States Figure Skating Association
("USFSA") are the property of USFSA and used herein by
permission of USFSA. All other rights reserved by USFSA. USFSA
assumes no responsibility for the contents of this book.

Series design: Barbara Berger

ISBN 0-553-48519-9

Published simultaneously in the United States and Canada

Bantam Books are published by Bantam Books, a division of
Bantam Doubleday Dell Publishing Group, Inc. Its trademark,
consisting of the words "Bantam Books" and the portrayal of a
rooster, is Registered in the U.S. Patent and Trademark Office and in
other countries. Marca Registrada. Bantam Books, 1540 Broadway,
New York, New York 10036.

PRINTED IN THE UNITED STATES OF AMERICA

OPM   0 9 8 7 6 5 4 3 2 1

1

"**V**eronica . . . *Veronica!*"

Corinne Carsen leaned back from the front passenger seat of the white Mercedes. She tapped Veronica Fouchard's Walkman headphones.

Veronica looked up. "What did you say, Corinne? I couldn't hear you over the music," she shouted.

"Could you please stop . . ." Mrs. Carsen started to shout back. She scowled and pulled off Veronica's headphones. They mussed the sixteen-year-old's shiny auburn hair.

"Could you please stop singing so loudly?" Mrs. Carsen said in a normal voice. "You're keeping Tori awake."

Tori squirmed on the other side of the backseat.

"It's okay, Mom. I can't sleep anyway," she said.

"Well, try," Mrs. Carsen said, facing forward again. "Tell her, Roger."

Tori sighed and waited for a lecture from her stepfather. But when Roger Arnold glanced in the rearview mirror from the driver's seat, his green eyes looked concerned.

"How do you feel, Tor?" he asked quietly.

Tori sighed again. Except for Veronica's off-key singing, the last hour in the car had been silent and miserable. Talking would be a relief.

"Truthfully? I feel tired and achy," Tori said. "And I can't stop thinking about what the doctor said."

"None of us can," Roger said. Tori saw Roger grip the steering wheel so tightly his knuckles turned white.

The four of them were speeding toward Philadelphia. Tori was about to compete in the National Figure Skating Championships, the biggest amateur figureskating competition in the United States. This should have been the happiest day of her life.

Instead, it was the worst.

That morning, Tori's doctor had told her she had a serious muscle disease. One that would slowly rob her body of strength.

One that might put her in a wheelchair forever.

One that would ruin her dream of skating for her country in the Olympics.

Tori pushed back a lock of her blond hair. She stared out the window, but she didn't see the beautiful ice-covered birch trees the car sped past.

Instead, she saw herself back in her Pennsylvania hometown, Seneca Hills, sitting across from Dr. Wyckoff.

The slender, brunette doctor had looked sad and serious. She had finally told Tori what was wrong—why Tori had felt so tired and achy and uncoordinated for the past weeks.

"You have myotonic muscular dystrophy," Dr. Wyckoff had explained.

Tori couldn't forget the way the doctor had kept tapping her pen nervously on her desk.

Suddenly a surprising thought jolted Tori.

"Mom?" she said. "What if Dr. Wyckoff is wrong? She's human. Maybe she messed those tests up. Or the lab did. Maybe I only have mono or something."

Mrs. Carsen turned around. Tori saw a flash of tears in her mother's blue eyes.

"You know I don't want you to skate at Nationals—" Mrs. Carsen said.

"Mom!" Tori cut in. "We went over all of that back at Dr. Wyckoff's office. I have to skate at Nationals. Now! While I still can!"

"Shhh." Mrs. Carsen leaned back and put a perfectly manicured finger to Tori's lips. "You didn't let me finish," she said.

Tori reached up and held her mother's cool hand.

"I was starting to say that I don't want you to skate. But you're fifteen now. That's old enough for you to make your own decision—even if I don't agree with it.

"I spoke to Dr. Wyckoff. It turns out there's a top

muscle specialist—Dr. Mitchell—at the university hospital in Philadelphia. He's booked for months. But you know me. I promise I'll get you an appointment with him."

Tori saw Roger glance at her mother, then stare ahead. His jaw muscle was twitching. Is he trying not to laugh? Tori wondered in surprise. What could he possibly think is funny about all this?

"Darling?" Roger said. "Did you tell the hospital you're *the* Corinne Carsen of Carsen Design Group?" He waggled his eyebrows.

Mrs. Carsen reached over and swatted Roger's arm lightly. "As a matter of fact, I did tell them," she said. "They weren't impressed. But what can you expect from people who wear white lab coats all day?"

She reached down and stroked the lapel of her sea green silk suit. Mrs. Carsen was a successful designer of very expensive clothes.

"Well, Corinne, when you married me, you got more than just the owner of Arnold's Department Store," Roger said. "I have some small amount of clout."

"Oh, please!" Veronica groaned from the backseat. "You sound like Donald Trump or something!"

"Hush up, Miss Smarty Pants," Roger said, frowning. But Tori could tell he was only pretending to be annoyed.

"I may not be Donald Trump," he continued, "but you three ladies are being chauffeured by a member of the university hospital's board of directors."

"Oh, my goodness! Darling! I forgot all about that!" Mrs. Carsen's face filled with hope. "You're on so many boards, I can't keep track of them all."

Veronica leaned forward and poked Roger's shoulder.

"Hey, chauffeur! I'm hungry," she said. "Could we stop for some food?"

Everyone laughed. Tori felt some of the awful, invisible weight on her shoulders ease up a little bit.

"If I had known you were calling the university hospital from Dr. Wyckoff's, I would have stopped you," Roger told Corinne. He slowed the car and pulled off the highway.

"Because while you were in Dr. Wyckoff's office using the phone, I was in the waiting room making an appointment for Tori on my cell phone. Dr. Mitchell is going to see Tori the day after tomorrow, on Monday morning. I didn't tell you right away because you were so upset."

Corinne reached over and stroked Roger's cheek. "Great minds think alike, darling," she said.

At the bottom of the exit ramp, Roger turned around and looked at Tori.

"Does that sound okay to you?" he asked.

"Yeah," Tori said. "It sounds really good." She was sure Dr. Mitchell would tell her it was all a mistake—that she didn't have MD.

"I'm starved!" Veronica piped up. "Let's eat."

Corinne glanced back at Veronica, then smiled at Roger.

"I'll tell you something else I never dreamed of when I married you," Corinne said. "I never dreamed I'd have another hungry teenager on my hands! But some people are just lucky, and I'm one of them."

"Oh, brother!" Veronica mumbled. But Tori could tell that Veronica was pleased. She was blushing slightly and trying not to smile.

Typical Veronica, Tori thought. Always trying to act cool and collected, like nothing affects her. But Veronica couldn't fool Tori anymore.

Veronica had moved in with the Carsens a few months earlier, right before Roger married Tori's mother. At first, Tori had resented her. Veronica was only a year older, but to Tori she seemed racy and dangerous. She broke every rule in the house without feeling the least bit guilty.

But Tori had discovered something else about Veronica. The sophisticated, sarcastic teenager also had a soft side.

"How about brown-rice sandwiches and salad?" Roger called out, breaking into Tori's thoughts. "There's a health food restaurant called Nature's Way just ahead."

"Health food?" Veronica said, wrinkling her small, perfectly straight nose. "Ick."

"Nature's Way sounds fine to me," Mrs. Carsen said. "That makes you the tiebreaker, Tori."

Tori glanced at Veronica, who tilted her head to the side and made a pleading face. Tori grinned.

"I vote for Nature's Way," Tori said.

"Traitor!" Veronica muttered. She was being her usual bratty self, but Tori didn't mind. It felt normal, and right now, normal felt good.

At the restaurant, they ordered their food to go. Veronica bought a sandwich, a health shake, and a salad. She also bought a carob bar. Back on the highway, Tori noticed that her mother and Roger were deep in a quiet conversation.

"I thought you hated health food," Tori said to Veronica.

"Mmmph. I do," Veronica said through a mouthful of her tofu-turkey sandwich. "But I was outvoted. And a person has to eat."

"Hey, Veronica?" Tori said quietly. "Thanks for what you did back at Dr. Wyckoff's."

Veronica waved her hand at Tori.

"All I said was that, if I were you, I'd skate at Nationals," Veronica said. "You have to go for it."

I do have to go for it, Tori thought. In her mind, she filled in the words Veronica *hadn't* said. I have to go for it, even if it's a big risk.

Dr. Wyckoff had said Tori could take a bad spill because of her weakened muscles. She'd also said Tori might find it hard to catch her breath after her rigorous routines.

Mrs. Carsen had begged Tori not to skate at Nationals. She didn't want Tori to hurt herself.

Tori glanced back at Veronica. "You supported me. And when I'm going against my mother, I need all the support I can get," she whispered.

"Well, you did the hard part," Veronica commented. "I never saw you stand up to your mom like that. It was pretty awesome."

Suddenly Tori felt protective of her mother. She gazed at her mother's profile as she leaned toward Roger, listening to him closely. Her blond hair, almost as light as Tori's, was swept into an elegant bun. She wore soft pink blush and lipstick.

She's so pretty, Tori thought. But she looks older. As if everything that's happened lately has aged her— from the day I fainted on the ice a couple of weeks ago to today, when Dr. Wyckoff gave us my diagnosis.

"Mom just doesn't want me to skate because she's scared," Tori said. "You know she gets overprotective."

"Hmph. You don't have to tell me," Veronica said with a snort. "She's the exact opposite of my mother."

Veronica looked out her window. Tori guessed that Veronica was thinking of her own mother. She lived in Paris and hardly ever contacted Veronica.

Tori leaned her head back on the leather seat. She suddenly felt exhausted. She closed her eyes and relaxed her body.

Minutes later she felt her muscles cramp up. She couldn't move!

Tori opened her mouth to scream for help, but she couldn't raise her voice above a whisper.

She tried to move her legs, but they felt as heavy as cement. She looked down and gasped. She was strapped into a wheelchair! The straps were wrapped around her legs, her lap, and her arms.

"*No!*" Tori screamed. "*No!*"

She struggled against the straps. They tightened around her arms as she pitched forward. She was falling!

"Tori!" a voice called her. "Tori! Wake up!"

Tori struggled to open her eyes. Her mother's concerned face was inches away. She was leaning all the way over the front seat, gripping Tori's arms tightly.

"Sweetheart," Mrs. Carsen said quietly. "Hush, now. You had a bad dream."

Tori sighed and leaned back. A bad dream. It was just a bad dream. She could still walk. And she could still skate.

But what if she really did have myotonic muscular dystrophy? She shivered despite the warm air in the car.

If she did, then going to the Olympics next month would never be more than a dream. But the nightmare she'd just had . . . the nightmare would become real.

Tori pulled her hair into a ponytail, then quickly washed her face and brushed her teeth. As she peered at herself in the bathroom mirror, she felt a shiver of excitement. Today was her first day of practice at Nationals! She had been working toward this competition since she was an eight-year-old with her first pair of skates.

In three days she would skate her short program. A few days after that, she would skate her long program. She felt a jolt of nerves just thinking about skating in front of an arena packed with television cameras, reporters, and thousands of spectators.

Tori walked back into the hotel bedroom she was sharing with Veronica. She tossed her bathrobe onto her bed.

Veronica moaned from the other bed.

"What time is it?" she croaked.

"Seven-thirty," Tori said. "Go back to sleep."

She walked to the window. Outside, the sun was just rising. It cast a cold, white winter light on the Delaware River. She held the windowsill for balance and stretched the backs of her legs. She felt an ache deep in her muscles. She wondered if it was a symptom of MD.

She wasn't going to let a little stiffness get in her way. After years of working through aches, pains, and colds, she knew how to push herself through practice.

She padded across the thick beige carpet and pulled open the closet door. The skating dresses she and her mother had hung there the night before were each covered in plastic and lined up neatly.

Back home, Tori was the best-dressed skater in her club, Silver Blades. It was one of the most prestigious figure-skating clubs in the country, but during practice, most kids wore casual clothes, such as leggings and sweats. Not Tori. Her mother told her that if she always dressed like a champion, she'd always skate like one.

But here at Nationals, Tori knew that all the competitors would dress up for practice. At this level of competition, it was important to look great. A judge could be watching at any time.

Tori knew that she would need more than fancy clothes to impress the judges, but it couldn't hurt that her mother designed all her costumes. They were beautiful and unique.

Tori ran her hand over the dresses. There were enough for a week of practices—a pink one with sequins, a white one with feathers, a blue one with a red sash that made it look military. The metal hangers chimed softly as Tori handled the dresses.

Veronica lifted her head from her pillow. Her short hair, usually brushed into a perfect bob, was sticking out around her head.

"Could you hold it down?" she snapped. "What are you doing, anyway? Playing cymbals or something?"

"Sorry," Tori said. "I'm just trying to pick out a dress for my first practice. Do you want to help?"

"Of course I do," Veronica muttered. "Right after I stick a hot poker in my eye." She disappeared under the bedspread.

Tori suddenly wished Natalia Cherkas were there. Natalia would help her pick out a dress. She loved Tori's clothes.

Natalia was a fourteen-year-old Russian skater who lived with the Carsens. She'd moved to the United States several months ago with her father, who was a busy diplomat in Washington, D.C. Her mother had died when she was very young.

Natalia also belonged to Silver Blades. Ambassador Cherkas had arranged to have her live with the Carsens. He wanted his daughter to have a family life while she skated for the club.

Tori and Natalia had become as close as sisters in the months since Natalia had moved in. Tori had been sad when Natalia told her she planned to stay with her father in Washington, D.C., for the week of Nationals. But Tori understood. She figured that Natalia was disappointed about not being able to skate in Nationals herself. She was still a Russian citizen and the rules said she couldn't compete for the United States. Being around Tori while she practiced and talked about the competition would probably have made Natalia unhappy and jealous, Tori realized.

Suddenly Tori felt Veronica standing right behind her.

"The purple one is nice," Veronica said. She ran her hand down the soft, velvety fabric. "But the stretchy pink one is kind of cute."

Tori smiled. She couldn't believe Veronica had actually gotten out of bed to help her.

"You're right," she said. "I like the pink one too."

Tori quickly pulled on the dress as Veronica climbed back into her warm bed. Tori tiptoed as she finished getting ready.

"For a dainty skater, you sound like an elephant when you walk around," Veronica complained.

"For someone who actually stayed in last night, you're pretty grumpy," Tori said. "What's your problem?"

"I don't have a problem," Veronica said. She rolled onto her stomach. "I just wish I didn't have to come to this boring ice-skating thing. I was supposed to go out with Evan this weekend."

Evan was Veronica's boyfriend. He was also the only person who could get her to smile on a daily basis. When Veronica was with Evan, she was sweet, funny, and glowing—the opposite of the way she usually acted.

Tori liked Evan, but she didn't think Veronica should be dating him. It was nothing against Evan— he was cute, funny, and nice. But Evan was twenty years old and he went to Seneca Hills Junior College. If Roger and Corinne found out Veronica was sneaking around with an older guy, they would have a fit. And Tori didn't like keeping secrets from them.

"You shouldn't be going out with him, anyway," Tori said. "If Evan finds out that you're sixteen, not eighteen like you said, he's going to dump you."

Veronica shrugged. "I have to chance it. Someday you'll meet someone who makes you feel as great as Evan makes me feel," she said. "Then you'll understand."

Tori rolled her eyes.

"Right, Veronica. You're such a woman of the world," Tori said. She rose on her tiptoes and squeezed her calf muscles. She bounced up and down a little. Her leg muscles—especially her feet—still felt really stiff.

I'll do lots of extra stretching before I hit the ice this morning, Tori thought. She wanted her muscles to be perfectly warmed up for her first practice at Nationals. She had to look strong in front of any judges who might be watching.

The phone rang.

Who could that be this early? Tori wondered.

The door to their bedroom opened a minute later. Roger walked in from the living room suite, which separated his and Mrs. Carsen's bedroom from the girls' room. He was wearing a terry-cloth bathrobe. He looked annoyed.

"There's someone named Evan on the phone," he said, frowning. He turned to Veronica, who sat up fast on her bed. "He wants to speak to you. Who is he?"

Veronica froze. Her mouth opened, but no words came out. Tori found herself feeling sorry for Veronica.

"He's—uh—he's—" Veronica stammered.

"That pain-in-the-neck reporter," Tori interrupted. Veronica turned to her, her brown eyes wide with surprise.

"A reporter?" Roger asked. "Why in the world would he want to talk to Veronica?"

"He's from a really bad paper—one of those supermarket tabloids," Tori said. "He's been trying to get an interview with me. I won't talk to him because he trashed another skater. So he started talking to Veronica, hoping he could get her to talk me into giving him an interview." Tori shrugged. "I'm sorry if he bothered you."

"Well, I can't have him harassing you—either of you," Roger said sternly. "I'll tell him—"

"No!" both girls shouted together. Roger paused, looking puzzled.

"I mean—let me talk to him myself," Tori said. "I'll really give him a piece of my mind!"

Roger looked doubtful, but Tori picked up the extension phone.

"Look, I told you I'm not giving you an interview!" she shouted. "Now, if I have to tell you again, my stepfather's going to call the police!"

Roger shook his head and left the room, closing the door behind him.

"Evan?" Tori said.

"Tori? Is that you?" Evan sounded confused. "What was that all about?"

"I'm so sorry! I thought you were someone else," Tori said. "Hold on, here's Veronica." She handed the phone to Veronica, who snatched it eagerly.

"Do you know what time it is? Why are you calling me here?" Veronica whispered. "You what? You missed me? Yeah. Me too."

Tori stuffed a hairbrush and socks into her skate bag, then glanced at Veronica. She had the phone cradled in her shoulder and she was smiling.

"Yeah. Double that." Veronica paused. "Hmmm. Triple that! Let me call you later, okay? I'll explain it all then," she said. She hung up the phone and glanced at Tori.

"Tor, you're a pal," she said. "That was really cool, you covering for me and all."

Tori shook her head. "I don't know why I did it," she said. "Nothing against Evan, but you should get a guy your own age."

"The guys my age are all childish jerks," Veronica said. "Anyway, thanks again."

Tori grabbed her skate bag and started for the door. As she gripped the handle, her finger muscles cramped up and then relaxed. She stopped dead. Why was this happening to her hand now? She shifted the bag to her other hand.

"Tori? Are you okay?" Veronica asked.

Tori flexed her hand. It felt better already. She just needed to do an extra-long stretching session at the rink, that was all.

"Yeah. I'm fine," Tori said. "See you later."

In the living room suite, Mrs. Carsen was sitting on the large floral-print couch. She was wearing a thick terry-cloth robe.

"Good morning," Mrs. Carsen said. She put down her newspaper.

"Hi, Mom," Tori said. "Why aren't you dressed? Practice is in half an hour."

"Dan is going to meet you in the lobby and take you over," Mrs. Carsen said. "I have some business to take care of here this morning."

Tori's mouth dropped open. She couldn't believe her mother wasn't going to her first practice at Nationals! She was glad Dan Trapp, her coach, was planning to meet her in the lobby. But she wanted her mother there, too.

Tori silently headed for the door.

"Wait!" Mrs. Carsen called.

Thank goodness! Tori thought with relief. Mom

changed her mind. She's going to ask me to wait while she gets dressed.

"Where do you think you're going without eating breakfast?" Mrs. Carsen said. She waved her hand at a silver tray on the coffee table. It held a plate of toast and a pitcher of orange juice.

Tori felt a surge of disappointment, and then one of anger, but she held her feelings in. She didn't want to waste her skating energy on an argument with her mother.

"I can't eat. I'm too excited, and I can't skate on a full stomach," she said.

Mrs. Carsen got up and strode over to Tori.

"Here," she said, thrusting a piece of whole wheat toast into Tori's hand. "At least eat this in the elevator."

Mrs. Carsen reached out and stroked Tori's cheek, but Tori turned her face away. Her mother looked hurt but didn't say anything.

"Have a great first practice, okay?" Mrs. Carsen said.

Tori nodded and quickly left the suite.

As she walked down the hall to the elevator, she realized that she was feeling sorry for herself. Natalia wasn't there to cheer her on. And now her mother wasn't coming to the most important practice of her life. The same mother who never gave her a minute of peace about her skating back home!

She doesn't want me to skate at Nationals, Tori realized. So she's not going to support me. She said she would, but she lied. Tori punched the elevator button hard.

Fine, she thought. I guess that means I'm on my own.

3

"Tori! Over here!" Dan Trapp called.

"Hi, Dan!" Tori waved. She crossed the marble lobby full of potted plants and leather furniture.

"Ready to get started?" Dan asked. The short, stocky coach gave her a quick hug.

"Ready and willing, Coach," she said, grinning.

"Where's skating mom number one?" Dan asked, looking behind Tori.

She felt her grin fade. "Mom's not coming."

"Oh," Dan said. "Well, let's get going then."

Tori could tell that Dan was surprised. Mrs. Carsen was known in Silver Blades as demanding and overbearing. She went to almost all of Tori's practices, and she often shouted out instructions and criticism to Tori from the side. Mrs. Carsen had been a skater herself once but had failed to reach the national level.

Tori and Dan stepped outside and onto the Philadelphia streets. The sidewalks had been shoveled, but there was still snow on the faces of the colonial brownstones they strolled past. The air was cool and crisp. The salt that had been spread on the sidewalks crunched under their feet.

"So, Tori, have you gotten your medical test results back yet?" Dan asked. He knew Tori had fainted on the ice a couple of weeks ago and then had gone to the doctor for all sorts of tests. But Dan didn't know that Dr. Wyckoff had called the Carsens into her office yesterday to deliver the terrible results.

Tori gulped. She hadn't thought about what she would tell Dan. She knew she couldn't tell him Dr. Wyckoff's diagnosis. What if Dan didn't want to coach a sick girl? A girl with myotonic muscular dystrophy?

"Um, we haven't gotten the results back yet," Tori said, feeling her face turn red as she told the lie.

"Well, I guess no news is good news, right?" Dan said with a grin. "How do you feel, anyway?"

"Fantastic," Tori said. Another lie. Her feet already hurt just from the walk!

At the arena, Dan and Tori entered through the double glass doors. They were hit by the noise of hundreds of people milling around the huge lobby. People stood in small circles, chatting. Others collected autographs from competitors. Others lugged skate bags and costumes wrapped in plastic bags.

"Look, Dan!" Tori cried.

She pointed to a banner stretched over the massive

doors to the rink. It read, WELCOME TO THE 1998 STATE FARM U.S. FIGURE SKATING CHAMPIONSHIPS!

Dan nodded and grinned. He gave Tori's arm a squeeze.

"Here we are, champ," he said.

Tori scanned the white walls of the lobby. They were covered with posters of skaters who had won at Nationals in the past. From where she stood, Tori could see posters of Rosalynn Sumners, Nancy Kerrigan, Brian Boitano, and Scott Hamilton. She got a shiver looking up at them.

Maybe my picture will be up there next year, she thought. A smile spread across her face.

She was jolted out of her dream by a finger tapping her shoulder.

"Hey, Tori Carsen! Can we have your autograph?" two voices said at the same time.

Tori spun around. Haley Arthur and Nikki Simon were standing there, grinning.

"Haley!" Tori cried. "Nikki!"

Haley and Nikki were members of Silver Blades, too. They weren't competing, but they had come to Nationals to cheer on Tori and Amber Armstrong. Amber was another Silver Blades member. She was only twelve, but she was a fantastic skater. She would give Tori some stiff competition.

"Haley!" Tori said. "You got your hair cut! What do you call that, um, *style*?"

Haley's red hair was cropped short, and it curled wildly.

"Excuse me for not looking like a Barbie doll," Haley said, grinning. "Anyway, Nikki likes it."

"On *you* I like it," Nikki Simon said, clutching her long light brown braid. "Don't get any ideas about cutting my hair, though!"

Dan cleared his throat loudly. "I hate to break up your reunion," he said, "especially since it's been at least a day since you've all seen each other. But I've got to go fill out some paperwork. Tori, how about if I meet you on the ice in fifteen minutes?"

"Sounds good, Dan," Tori said. The coach walked off, and Tori turned back to her friends.

"Look who's here!" Haley yanked a girl with jet-black hair into the center of the group.

"Jill!" Tori screamed. She grabbed her friend and they hugged each other hard. Jill Wong had been a member of Silver Blades for years. Then she had transferred to the International Ice Academy in Colorado. She hardly ever got to see the girls from Silver Blades anymore. They all kept in touch by phone and letters.

"It's so great to see your smiling face," Tori said. "I hope you brought pictures of Jesse," she added. Everyone knew that Jill had a new boyfriend, Jesse Barrow.

"Tori!" A voice piped up. They all turned to see a tiny girl with light brown hair speeding toward them.

"Hey, it's Amber, the mini-Tori," Haley teased. Amber idolized Tori. She copied Tori's every move and hung around her like a shadow. When she wasn't competing against her on the ice, that is.

"Me? The mini-Tori?" Amber smirked at Haley. "If you're saying my triple toe loop is as good as Tori's, then I guess you're right."

"*Almost* as good," Tori said, her eyes narrowing. "But not quite. Not if you know what's good for you!"

Everybody laughed and started chattering at once.

"So how *is* Jesse?" Tori asked, grinning at Jill.

Jill blushed as red as her favorite practice sweater. "He's really great," she said with a dreamy smile.

"First he was your best friend. Now he's your boyfriend," Haley teased.

"Mmm, sounds perfect," Tori sighed. "I wish my mom would let me date."

"Where is your mother, anyway?" Jill asked.

"She couldn't come," Tori complained. "She said she had something to take care of this morning. I don't know if it has something to do with her clothing business. To tell you the truth, I was so mad, I didn't ask her for an explanation."

"You have got to be kidding! *Your* mom isn't coming to your first practice at Nationals?" Jill was amazed. "Your mom's been at every practice since you were learning how to lace your skates!"

"I'm surprised she's not coming just to make sure you don't pass out again," Haley pointed out. All Tori's friends in Silver Blades had been there when she fainted on the ice.

"Passed out?" Jill's face showed surprise, then concern. She turned to Tori. "You fainted?"

Tori waved her hand at Jill. "Please! I got a little woozy is all. I was hungry. Then Mom flipped out completely. She even dragged me to the doctor!"

"And we all know how much you love the doctor," Nikki said.

"Yup," Tori agreed. "The doctor's office is my favorite place on the planet. I adore being prodded with freezing-cold instruments. And those needles! There's nothing like a good injection!"

Nikki, Haley, and Jill giggled, and Tori joined in. Inside, though, Tori felt miserable. She hated lying to her good friends. But Tori wasn't going to tell anyone that she might have MD. She couldn't afford to appear weak. Not even in front of her friends!

The girls strolled into the rink area. They stood watching the skaters who were already warming up and practicing their routines.

"Oh, Jill, look. There's your roommate now," Haley said. They all glanced at the ice in time to see Carla Benson leap into a flawless triple flip.

"Ugh!" Jill made a face. "The evil ice princess herself. I'm really enjoying this vacation away from her. I still have to see her at practice, but at least I don't have to share a room with her."

Carla had been accepted into the International Ice Academy a few months earlier. She was Jill's roommate there. Carla was a good skater, good enough to be competing at Nationals. But Carla also went out of her way to upset other skaters before a competition. Jill had almost lost her concentration at Sectionals because Carla hinted that Jesse Barrow had asked her on a date.

Carla's blond hair was pulled into a shiny, bouncing ponytail. Her workout clothes were almost as elaborate as Tori's. But where Tori's dresses were elegant, Carla's were flashy. Today she had on a dress that looked like a space suit. It was silver with shiny metal buttons at the shoulders.

The girls from Silver Blades watched as Carla stroked backward halfway around the rink until she was near them. Then she twirled into a tight, fast spin with her arms crossed over her chest. As she came out of it, she skated in a large circle, smiling brilliantly and tossing her ponytail. Almost as an afterthought, Carla hitched herself into a flawless triple toe loop.

"Give me a break," Haley moaned.

"Could she be a bigger show-off?" Nikki added.

"She *is* a natural skater," Tori admitted.

The other girls turned slowly toward her.

"*You're* complimenting Carla?" Haley said.

"I didn't compliment her," Tori said with a sniff. "I said she was a natural skater. And she is. Naturally nasty. Anyway, you should see that girl's sit spin. She looks like a wobbly gyroscope! I'm going to enjoy beating the skates off her."

Out of the corner of her eye, Tori saw her friends exchange knowing glances. She knew how she ap-

peared to them. She was the same old Tori—competi-
tive, confident, and cool. But she didn't *feel* like the
same old Tori. She was hiding something from her
closest friends. She was hiding the fact that she might
have a serious disease. One that was making it harder
and harder for her to skate.

Tori knew she could have beaten Carla a few
months ago. But that was when she was at the top of
her form.

Lately, there were days when just walking made her
tired.

How could she beat Carla now?

"No, no, no!" Dan yelled across the ice. "Keep your arms tucked in!"

Tori bit her lip and felt tears burning her eyelids. Dan had *never* yelled at her before. He was the kind of laid-back coach who told skaters that trying hard was good enough. And she was trying. She was using every ounce of energy she had, but she was dragging through her routine. Her leg muscles were crying out for her to stop skating.

She glanced around quickly to see if any of the other skaters had heard her coach screaming at her. No one was paying attention, she realized with relief.

"Try it again, Tori. Focus!" Dan called. His voice echoed off the nearly empty bleachers in the huge arena.

She shook her head and took a deep breath. She

struck the opening pose of her short program. As she began stroking, Dan yelled, "Stop!"

She couldn't believe it. What had come over Dan? Was he as nervous about Nationals as she was? He would be even more nervous if he knew she might be sick. She was glad she hadn't told him the truth about her diagnosis.

She glided over to Dan, who was standing near the boards, frowning.

"Hey, champ," Dan said. "Sorry I lost my cool there. I guess the pressure is getting to me."

Tori smiled. "It's okay," she said. "It's getting to me, too. Maybe you should practice one of your relaxation exercises." She giggled. Dan used some unusual coaching methods. One of them called for skaters to relax by picturing themselves as melting butter or waves in the ocean or some other goofy thing.

"That's not a bad idea," Dan said. "In fact, maybe we should both practice relaxing. You look a little tired, so let's call it a morning. We can meet back here this afternoon."

"But Dan," Tori complained, "I still haven't gotten all the way through my short program." Tori's muscles were aching, but she didn't want to stop. At least ten of the other skaters she would compete against were still on the ice, working hard.

"Tor, you look tired. You're not focusing," Dan said. "Trust me, it's time to call it a morning."

She frowned, but she knew better than to argue with him. He was easygoing, but he was also stubborn. She stepped off the ice. Dan handed over her skate guards, and she slipped them on.

Nothing is going right today, she thought. *Nothing.* She turned around and looked back at the ice. Jill was on the opposite end of the rink, holding her leg high in a graceful spiral. Amber was launching into a triple salchow. The young girl landed the jump flawlessly.

I don't stand a chance, Tori thought miserably. I never should have come here!

Tori slipped her key into the door back at the hotel. She could hear voices inside. She stepped into the living room suite just as a voice yelled, "Tori!"

"Nat!" Tori screamed. "What are you doing here?"

The two girls hugged for a long minute. Tori looked over Natalia's shoulder and saw her mother sitting on the couch with a pleased smile on her face.

"I thought you were staying with your dad," Tori said. "What happened?"

"I could not keep away," Natalia said. "Even though I knew you wanted me to."

"What?" Tori said, shocked. "What are you talking about? Why would I want you to keep away?"

Natalia looked puzzled.

"Because I would be the—what do you call it? The party pooper. I thought you would always be trying to cheer me up because I can't skate at Nationals. But I didn't want you to have to worry about me."

"Nat!" Tori exclaimed, hugging the other girl again. "I was dying to have you come. But I thought you weren't coming because you would be too sad, watching *me* get ready to compete."

"Why would that make me sad?" Natalia said. "I want to help you!"

"Thank goodness!" Tori said. "I want you to help me. No offense to Veronica, but you can imagine how good she is at that!"

"How good I am at what?" Veronica asked, walking from their bedroom into the living room.

"Never mind!" Tori and Natalia said at the same time.

Mrs. Carsen laughed. "Now do you see why I couldn't come to your first practice?" she asked. "Natalia called last night. She asked if I could pick her up at the train station and bring her back here this morning. I would have asked Roger to do it, but you know he's visiting an old college friend this morning."

"Oh, Mom!" Tori cried. "I was so mad at you. I didn't know why you weren't coming."

Tori ran to the couch and gave her mother a hug. She felt great all of a sudden. She turned toward Veronica, but the older girl raised one hand.

"Don't hug me," Veronica said. She picked up a magazine from the coffee table and started thumbing through it.

"Well, now you know why I didn't come," Mrs. Carsen said. "I wanted Natalia's arrival to be a surprise. It seemed like something that would cheer you up."

"It did," Tori said. She flopped onto the couch between Veronica and her mother. "And just in time," she added, thinking of her miserable practice that morning.

Natalia instantly understood what Tori meant. "How *was* your first practice?" she asked.

"Not so good," Tori said. "I'm really stiff and tired. Dan actually yelled at me."

"*Dan* yelled?" Natalia asked. "That must have been something to hear!"

"Well, I never want to hear it again," Tori said. "But I have a feeling Dan is as nervous as I am. Come to practice this afternoon. You'll see what I mean."

"I plan to come to practice this afternoon," Natalia said. "And to all your practices."

"Oh, Nat," Tori said. "I am so glad you're here. Did I tell you that already?"

"Yes, but a person can hear that kind of thing more than once," Natalia said, grinning. "Come on. Help me unpack."

"Unpack?" Veronica said. "Where are you going to be sleeping?"

Mrs. Carsen cleared her throat. "I've already called the front desk. They're sending up a cot for your room."

"I am *not* sleeping on a cot," Veronica said.

"I'll sleep on it," Natalia offered.

"Don't be ridiculous, Natalia," Mrs. Carsen said. "We're so glad you gave up this time with your father just to come and be with Tori. You'll sleep on one of the beds."

"But Tori can't sleep on the cot!" Natalia said. "She needs her rest." Natalia had gone with Tori to Dr. Wyckoff's office the day before. She knew about the MD diagnosis.

"True," Mrs. Carsen said.

Veronica groaned and threw down the magazine.

"I can't believe it," she said. "First I'm stuck at this ice nightmare, and now I have to sleep on a cot? Life is so unfair." She stomped back into the bedroom.

Tori smiled at Natalia and her mother. They were both smiling back. The morning had started out terribly, but now things were looking up. Maybe, just maybe, everything was going to turn out all right.

5

It was dark when Tori and Mrs. Carsen parked outside the university hospital on Monday morning. Roger, Veronica, and Natalia were still sleeping back at the hotel.

Tori and her mother walked in silence through the parking lot, shivering against the cold winter wind. They paused at the doors of the huge glass-and-concrete building.

"Ready?" Mrs. Carsen said.

Tori nodded. They pushed through the doors.

Inside, several long white-tiled halls led off the lobby. Nurses and doctors bustled back and forth. Loud announcements sounded over hidden speakers.

Tori scurried down the hall behind her mother. She already hated the big city medical center. It was so cold-looking—nothing like Dr. Wyckoff's comfortable, wood-paneled office. But maybe that was good, Tori thought. Maybe bigger meant better. Maybe the hospital was more efficient and scientific than Dr. Wyckoff's family practice. Tori hoped so.

She and her mother finally found the right office. The door had a brass plaque with the name Edward Mitchell, M.D. They pushed through the door. Tori and her mother stood uncertainly in the small, empty waiting room.

A young man in jeans and a button-down shirt was sitting at the reception desk.

"Tori?" he said. "Mrs. Carsen?"

"Yes," Tori said, surprised. She guessed the receptionist had been expecting them.

"Thanks for coming in. I'm Dr. Mitchell."

Tori felt her mouth dropping open, but she quickly snapped it shut. She looked at her mother. Mrs. Carsen was staring wide-eyed at the doctor.

He grinned at them. He had sandy-blond hair and a goatee. "I look a lot younger than I am," he said. "Follow me."

They walked behind the doctor into his office. On his desk, Tori could see a framed snapshot of him rock climbing.

"Thank you for seeing us," Mrs. Carsen said. "I understand that you are the best in your field."

"How nice of you to say so." Dr. Mitchell smiled again.

Tori grinned nervously. This didn't feel like a doctor's visit. It felt like a social call!

"Dr. Wyckoff has faxed me the tests and their results," Dr. Mitchell said. His manner was suddenly sober. "I'm afraid I have to agree with Dr. Wyckoff's diagnosis. According to these results, Tori has myotonic muscular dystrophy."

Tori gasped. Her heart thundered in her ears. The doctor was still talking, but she couldn't hear him. She fought to take a deep breath. Did this mean the diagnosis was final? Did she absolutely, positively have MD? She glanced at her mother.

Mrs. Carsen's eyes were fixed on the doctor in a cold stare. "Well, perhaps you should look the tests over again." She leaned forward, frowning.

Dr. Mitchell cocked his head slightly. He put down the folder with Tori's results in it.

"Mrs. Carsen, I understand that this is upsetting for you and Tori. But the best thing to do right now is probably—"

"*I* will say what is best," Mrs. Carsen spat. Her jaw jutted out. Her voice became deep and harsh. "What is best now is for you to give Tori those tests again. Obviously the lab in Seneca Hills performed the tests wrong. But I expect more from a large institution like yours! *Far* more! Perhaps the problem here is that we need a specialist who's been in practice for a little bit longer."

Tori cringed as her mother lectured the young doctor. But she kept quiet. Her mother knew how to run things. If this was how she planned to get results, Tori wasn't going to stop her. Maybe her mother was right. Maybe this doctor was too young to know what he was doing.

"Naturally I had already planned to readminister the tests," Dr. Mitchell said. He held his hands up, as if he had to defend himself from Mrs. Carsen.

"Doctor?" Tori finally spoke up. "Could those test results from home be wrong?"

Dr. Mitchell gazed at Tori.

"Yes," he finally said. "They *could* be, but—"

Mrs. Carsen cut him off again.

"Those test results *are* wrong," she said. "You just make sure you're more careful than Dr. Wyckoff and her labful of idiots. Am I clear?"

Dr. Mitchell sighed. "You are crystal clear, Mrs. Carsen."

Tori's head was spinning. What did it all mean? *Were* the tests wrong?

She cleared her throat.

"I have another question," Tori said. The doctor stared at her.

"My question is, can I still skate? I'm supposed to be competing here at Nationals."

Dr. Mitchell smiled softly. He had a kind face.

"Tori, if you feel up to skating, you should go ahead. I don't know a lot about skating, but even I've heard of Nationals. I know it's a big deal," he said. "Do you feel up to it?"

Tori felt tears come to her eyes. She forced herself to

blink them back. She wouldn't cry now! She couldn't look weak in front of the doctor. He might change his mind about her skating.

"Yes," Tori lied. "I feel up to it."

"Don't you worry about what my daughter feels up to," Mrs. Carsen said through her teeth. "You just call the lab and tell them we're coming down. I want those tests given right away. We don't have all day."

6

"This is it, Tori," Dan Trapp said. "One-third of your score."

It was Wednesday morning, the day of the short program. Tori stood near the opening in the boards. Dan was squeezing a knot out of one of her shoulders. He was giving her a pep talk at the same time.

"Lucky for us, Cara Hopkins isn't here because of her sprained ankle. She would have given you some major competition.

"But you're still up against some of the biggest skaters," Dan continued. "Amber, Jill, Carla. You know they're good. You've also got to beat Tracy Wilkins and Fiona Bartlet.

"But I've seen you skate better than all of them," he added. "If you concentrate and give it your all, you'll easily finish in the top three."

Tori nodded. She was listening to Dan. But she also kept thinking about what results would come from the latest batch of medical tests. She forced herself to concentrate on what Dan was saying.

"Go warm up. Don't use too much energy practicing your jumps. Nail them and quit," Dan said. He gave her a light push toward the ice.

Tori was in the final group of skaters warming up on the ice. Jill and Carla were there too. Jill wore a soft pink chiffon dress with flowing cap sleeves and a laced bodice. Carla was in a tight white dress with purple feathers. Tori smoothed her blue satin dress and fluffed out the short, lacy skirt.

She skated around the rink, trying to get her muscles warm. It took several trips. Soon she was stroking smoothly and powerfully. She felt a surge of hope. Maybe she'd skate her short program well, even though she felt rotten. When the five-minute warm-up ended, Tori skated off the ice.

Dan Trapp took her aside and held both of her hands.

"Go find a private place to focus," he ordered. "Relax, and picture your short program in your mind. See yourself skating every move perfectly. Okay?"

Tori nodded.

"I'll see you right before you step on the ice," Dan said.

Tori walked to the cavernous backstage area of the arena. She found a quiet corner and dragged over a metal folding chair. She plunked down and took a deep breath. She pictured her routine. She saw herself moving through the spins and jumps to her music.

She felt a nervous hum in her stomach. She was slightly queasy, but excited too. It was a familiar feeling. She got it before every competition.

Tori tried not to dwell on how important the short program was. But she couldn't block out her nervous thoughts. The short program called for her to complete several required elements, including a double axel and lots of fancy footwork. Would she be strong enough for the jump? Would her muscles be loose enough for her to make her footwork look graceful and coordinated? She felt her stomach cramp up in knots.

Mrs. Carsen walked in and sat next to Tori. She smoothed Tori's hair with her long, cool fingers.

"Relax, Tori," her mother said.

Tori folded her arms and took several deep breaths. She never watched the skaters who went ahead of her. It was too nerve-racking. But the sounds of the first skater's music filtered into the room.

Tori recognized it as Carla's piece. She knew that Carla's flashy style would show through in everything she did. All her moves had a flourish, and she always shot confident smiles at the judges. She was like a cheerleader.

Next came Jill's music. Tori had seen Jill's newest short program. If Tori hadn't been so nervous, she would have loved seeing it again. Jill's long legs and quiet confidence made her skating look like a ballet solo. Everything she did looked easy—even her triple Lutz–double toe loop.

Dan appeared at the entrance of the backstage area. He pointed to his watch.

"It's time, Tori," he called.

Tori sighed and stood up. Her mother stood too.

"I'll be watching with Dan," Mrs. Carsen said. "Good luck, sweetheart."

Tori walked over to Dan. Her coach put his arm around her as they made their way to the rink.

"Take it easy, Tori," Dan said. "Have some fun out there. I've seen you do this program beautifully a hundred times. Today doesn't have to be different."

As Tori and Dan walked closer to the rink, her old confidence came back. The cool air of the rink, the heaviness of her skates, even the butterflies in her stomach—it all felt familiar. This was her life. Skating was all she knew, and she loved it.

Tori took a deep breath and peered around the arena. Crowds of people packed the bleachers, chattering and rustling their programs. Television cameras pointed at the well-lit ice.

"Tori!" a reporter called. "Over here!"

Dan waved the reporter off. Tori ducked her head and kept walking toward the opening in the boards. She pulled off her skate guards and handed them to Dan.

"Good luck," he said. He squeezed Tori's hand. "Knock 'em dead."

Tori put the television cameras and judges out of her mind. It was time to focus. The announcer called her name. Tori skated to center ice to the sound of applause. She thought she could hear Natalia shouting, "Go, Tori!"

Tori struck her opening pose. The strains of Jacques Offenbach's "Gaîté Parisienne" began. Tori loved the bouncy, fun piece of music. One part sounded as if a row of cancan dancers were about to leap onto the ice with her.

Tori began with lively opening steps, followed by a double axel. She held the landing until she was sure every judge had seen.

She realized that she hadn't been smiling when she landed the jump. Concentrate! she told herself. She pumped her legs in powerful back crossovers, with a few turns and an arabesque, until she was at the other end of the rink. Now it was time for a tough combination jump: a triple Lutz–double toe loop. Tori nailed the combination. Yes! she thought. She sailed through the Mohawk turns that brought her around the rink again.

She was breathing heavily by this time. It's too early to be tired, she thought. What if I've used up all my energy?

She tried to control her breathing. She tightened her body and threw herself into a layback spin. She came out of the spin and did two back crossovers. Then she stretched her leg back for an intricate spiral sequence.

Next came her spin combination. Spins didn't get the audience as excited as spectacular jumps did, but they were difficult. Especially when you're tired, she thought. Tired and maybe really sick.

Suddenly Tori pictured Dr. Mitchell, with his goatee and young face. She could hear him telling her that she had myotonic muscular dystrophy.

MD.

I have MD.

I shouldn't even be out here! she thought.

She wobbled as she lowered herself into a sit spin. Then she did a back sit spin. With a flourish, she stood and grabbed her left foot, pulling it high over her head.

The crowd applauded enthusiastically. Didn't they see how sloppy my sit spin was? Tori thought. I can't mess up like that again!

She stroked down the ice, breathing heavily but forcing herself to smile. At the other end of the rink she got ready for her triple loop. She hurled herself into the jump.

It was wrong from the start. She could feel it. She didn't have enough height in her jump. In a split second, she had to decide whether to turn the triple into a double . . . or hit the ice with a thud on her behind.

She did both.

She heard the crowd gasp as she fell. The jarring

thud jangled her teeth together. She blinked hard against the pain and popped right up. She smiled and moved smoothly back into her routine.

But she wanted to cry. She wanted to skate off the ice. She wanted her mother to hug her and tell her everything would be all right.

She did a straight-line step sequence, including bracket hops, choctaws, and twizzles. She forced herself to keep smiling as she hopped along with cancan-like kicks.

The last fifteen seconds went by in slow motion. She knew she had to end on a high note. She finished with a flying camel, which she hit perfectly.

The crowd clapped loudly. Tori bowed and waved. She skated toward the boards.

She had nailed most of her moves, except for the awful triple loop and the sloppy sit spin. But she had been concentrating so hard, she had forgotten to feel the music. And she hadn't made a connection with the audience and the judges. Her usual sparkle had been missing.

Tori stopped at the opening in the boards and stepped off the ice. Dan smiled encouragingly. She grabbed his hand and her mother's. The three of them walked to the area called the kiss-and-cry, where skaters waited for their scores.

Tori and Dan sat on the small bench as Mrs. Carsen stood nearby. Tori watched the electronic scoreboard anxiously. She was still breathing hard and her legs were starting to cramp up.

The numbers finally flashed across the board. Tori was in third place. She knew she should be glad. It was a good score, considering the competition she was up against. But Amber still hadn't skated. If Amber got a higher score, Tori would be knocked into fourth place.

She tried to smile. She was painfully aware of the looming television cameras pointing at her face. Dan squeezed her hand.

"That's a very good score," he said quietly. "Don't worry about not placing first. You're still in the running."

The applause faded and the next skater began. Dan put an arm around Tori and looked into her eyes.

"Are you sure you're feeling all right?" he asked.

"Didn't you just tell me my scores were good?" Tori asked.

"The scores were fine. Your skating was fine. But I saw you breathing hard, sweating. You looked exhausted out there. And you were concentrating so hard on your program, you forgot you were performing for an audience, too."

"I know that already, Dan," Tori snapped.

He sighed. "Look, I don't want to bug you. But since you fainted in Seneca Hills, I've been worried."

Tori didn't know what to say. She hadn't realized Dan was worried about her. But she couldn't tell him the truth now.

"Dan, I went to the doctor this morning. He gave me a clean bill of health. He says I'm fine!"

She grinned at him, feeling bad about the whopping lie.

She looked up and saw that her mother was standing just behind Dan. Mrs. Carsen's forehead wrinkled and she shook her head slowly. Tori shot her mother a warning look.

Mrs. Carsen forced herself to smile as she walked up to Tori and squeezed her tightly.

"That's right," she told Dan. "Tori's doing fine."

Dan nodded, but he didn't look convinced.

"I've got to go prepare Amber for her program," he said. "I'll call you tonight at the hotel, Tori."

Mrs. Carsen turned back to Tori. Her smile faded away.

"Come with me," she said. She hurried Tori to a private corner in the locker room.

"Sit down," she commanded. "Let me feel your muscles." She ran her hands down Tori's legs, massaging them. "You're as hard as a rock. You're stiff, tight, and exhausted." She sighed. "Whatever you have, it's really robbing you of your strength."

Tori twirled her ankle slowly and winced. Her muscles felt like iron. But her mother's words rang in her ears.

"Whatever you have," she had said. Her mom knew that *something* was wrong. But she didn't believe Tori had muscular dystrophy.

Her right calf seized up into a painful spasm. She reached down to massage it herself. As she did, she realized something frightening.

Maybe Mom's right, and I don't have MD. But there's something very wrong with me. And if it gets any worse, I'm not just going to mess up my long program on Saturday. I'm not even going to be able to finish it!

7

"**Y**es, I will!" Tori shouted.

"No, you will not!" Mrs. Carsen shouted back.

"It's not fair," Tori said. "Everyone else is going. *Everyone*. What's the point of being at Nationals if I can't even have some fun with my friends?"

Tori stomped across the living room and threw herself into an armchair.

"The point of being here is to compete," Mrs. Carsen said. "You're not here to socialize."

"I'm not asking if I can stay out all night, Mom!" Tori cried. "I just want to go have hot chocolate with my friends at the arena."

"You heard me, Tori," her mother said. "We have to be at Dr. Mitchell's office at the crack of dawn tomorrow. You need your rest. You're going to take a hot bath and go to bed early tonight."

Roger had been standing beside the large windows in the living room, looking at the view of the Delaware River. He turned around and cleared his throat.

"Tori? Will you go to your room, please?"

Tori turned toward Roger, stunned.

"What?" she said. "Are you punishing me?"

"Just go to your room, please," Roger repeated.

Tori pushed herself out of the chair. Her feet twinged as she put her weight on them. She marched to the door of her room. Then she turned around and glared at Roger. She could feel tears of anger coming to her eyes.

"You're not my father!" she screamed.

Roger's face fell. Tori felt a rush of satisfaction. Good, she thought. That's what he gets for ordering me around. She walked into the bedroom and slammed the door.

Natalia looked up from the book she was reading in bed.

"Did you hear all that?" Tori asked.

Natalia nodded.

"Well, you should still go meet everyone. Just because I have to stay in my room like a little baby doesn't mean you can't go have some fun," Tori said. She hurled herself onto the other bed.

"No. I don't want to go without you," Natalia said.

"Are you *both* nuts?" Veronica said. She was sitting cross-legged on her cot applying shiny white nail polish. The phone sat right next to her. She had been waiting for Evan to call for the last hour.

"What do you mean?" Natalia asked.

"Well," Veronica said, "Tori is nuts because she's making such a big deal out of having hot chocolate with her babyish friends. And you're nuts, Natalia, because you want to stay here and be miserable with Tori when you could go out and have some fun."

"You mean, have some fun with my *babyish* friends?" Tori snapped.

"Hey! Don't take your tantrum out on me," Veronica said. She blew on her nails.

Tori rubbed her eyes. She felt tired and depressed. Amber had placed first in the short program earlier that day. Her score had knocked Tori into fourth place. Tori knew she should be glad Amber had skated well. Instead, she just felt disappointed about her own fourth-place finish.

Tori turned back to Natalia.

"Go, Nat. Everybody's going to be there—Nikki, Jill, Haley, Amber. They're all going to watch the ESPN rebroadcast of the short programs. They're showing them on the big screen in the lobby of the arena."

"It's okay," Natalia said. "This book is really good."

"Really?" Veronica said. "That looks like a biology textbook to me."

Natalia slid the book under the covers. "Never mind," she said. "I want to stay here with Tori."

There was a soft knock on the door.

"Who could that be?" Veronica asked. "Could it be Prince Charming? Come in, Prince!"

Roger opened the door and poked his head in.

"Tori? I'm sorry if you thought I was trying to boss you around. Can I come in?" His face looked so sad, Tori felt guilty about what she had said before.

"Come in," she said. "I'm sorry I yelled at you."

Roger walked over to the bed and sat next to Tori.

"I just wanted you to leave the room so I could calm your mom down a little bit," he said. "Maybe get her to see a little reason."

"Ha!" Tori sniffed. "Fat chance of that. When Mom makes up her mind, that's that."

"We-ell, not always," Roger said, grinning.

"You mean . . . ," Tori said, sitting up.

"Yup," Roger said. "You can go. But be home by nine-thirty."

"Roger! You are the best stepfather ever!" Tori said. She launched herself into his arms and gave him a tight hug. Then she kissed both his cheeks.

Roger untangled himself from her grip and stood up.

"For a stepdaughter, you're not so bad yourself," he said.

"What about me?" Veronica said from the cot.

"You'll do," Roger said. He ducked out of the room just as Veronica threw a pillow at him.

On Thursday morning Dr. Mitchell sat stiffly at his desk in front of Tori and Mrs. Carsen. He fingered a bright yellow folder. Tori could see her name written on the label.

Tori glanced at her mother. She sat in a modern leather chair. Her pink suit was crisp. Her blond hair was pulled into a prim chignon. She looked calm. Tori took a deep breath and crossed her legs exactly like her mother. It made her feel better.

"Mrs. Carsen, Tori. I've got the new test results back," Dr. Mitchell said in a low voice. "I'm afraid—" he paused. "I'm afraid the results were no different than before. The diagnosis is that Tori has myotonic muscular dystrophy."

Tori gasped. She hadn't realized how tightly she had

been gripping her chair. Now she tried to stand up. But she couldn't make her left hand let go of the chair.

"My hand!" she cried.

Dr. Mitchell stood and walked around his desk. He slowly uncurled Tori's fingers from the chair's arm.

"That's part of the MD," he said quietly. "Your hands may have a delayed ability to unclasp things. It will feel like a spasm."

Tori shook her head. "It can't be," she said. Tears sprang to her eyes. She started to stand up, but she couldn't see anything. She sank back into the chair.

"It can't be," she said again. She felt tears trickling down her cheeks. She gasped for breath.

She had been so hopeful that the first test results were wrong. But how could there be any doubt now? She even had the symptoms. She couldn't make her hand let go of the chair.

She wiped her eyes and glanced at her mother. What was she supposed to do now?

Mrs. Carsen was staring at Dr. Mitchell. Her eyes were slowly growing wider. But her mouth was getting tighter and tighter.

"I've spoken to Dr. Wyckoff," Dr. Mitchell continued. "Tori, you're quite young. Based on that, we have to assume that you've got a somewhat severe case."

A somewhat severe case. Suddenly Tori felt angry. Her eyes fell on the picture on Dr. Mitchell's desk— the one that showed him rock climbing. He didn't have any kind of disease. He was young and healthy. After he told Tori she had a "somewhat severe case" of MD, he could forget all about her and go rock climbing!

Who did he think he was?

Tori didn't want to hear another word. She wanted to get up and run out of the room. She wished she could pick up a remote, change the channel, and make Dr. Mitchell go away forever. But nothing would change the diagnosis.

"The next course of action is to make a decision about how to handle the effects of this disease. Tori, you need to start watching carefully to see which muscle groups are being affected."

Tori shivered. She looked at her mother again. Say something, Mom! she thought.

Mrs. Carsen was shaking her head. Sweat beaded on her upper lip.

The doctor bowed his head. "I'm very sorry to have to tell you this."

"You!" Mrs. Carsen finally spat. "You should be reported to the American Medical Association! How dare you tell my daughter she has muscular dystrophy? How dare you frighten her like that?"

"Mrs. Carsen, I had all the tests run twice. These are the correct results. I'm basing my diagnosis on them."

"Why should I rely on a diagnosis from you?" Mrs. Carsen said coldly. "You're probably not even old enough to vote."

Mrs. Carsen grabbed her purse from the floor. She pulled out a tissue, wiping carefully at Tori's eyes.

"Come on, sweetheart," Mrs. Carsen said. "We're leaving now."

"Wait, Mom. I want—I need—I have to—" Tori stammered. She swallowed hard and tried to control her emotions.

"Dr. Mitchell, am I going to die?" she choked out.

Dr. Mitchell shook his head. "Someday, just like all of us. But you're not going to die of muscular dystrophy. Most people with this disease have a normal life span."

"Then how long do I have before I'm—you know. Before I have to be in a wheelchair all the time?"

"It's hard to tell, Tori. It could be as early as a few months. It could be years from now. I just can't answer that."

Tori gulped. "Is there any medication I can take to slow it down? Maybe if I had some kind of massage therapy or—what do you call it?—acupuncture. Is there anything that will keep it from happening so fast?"

"Well . . ." Dr. Mitchell's voice was doubtful. "We don't really have any completely reliable drug therapies for muscular dystrophy. As for alternative medicine, I just don't know. But truthfully, I haven't seen any evidence that alternative treatments help much."

"Then there's no cure?" Tori asked.

"No." Dr. Mitchell shook his head.

Tori buried her head in her hands. Sobs shook her body.

Mrs. Carsen reached over and grabbed Tori's hand.

"That's enough, Doctor," she said coldly. "Do you see what you've done?" She turned toward Tori. "Let's go, sweetheart. I've heard just about enough here."

"Wait, Mom," Tori said. "I have one more question. I want to know if I can still skate. My long program at Nationals is in a few days."

"I can't answer that question for you," Dr. Mitchell said gently. "We don't know enough about this disease. But you could suffer from a muscle spasm and fall and hit your head. Or any number of things could happen. There is a real risk, Tori. But—"

"But as long as I feel up to it . . . ," Tori interrupted.

Dr. Mitchell shook his head. "What I'm saying, Tori, is that it's your choice."

Tori turned to her mother. Mrs. Carsen's eyes were grim. She clutched her purse tightly.

"Can I, Mom?" Tori said quietly.

"We don't have to talk about that now, Tori," Mrs. Carsen said. "But we do have to go."

Mrs. Carsen hooked her arm through Tori's. She led her out of the hospital. The sun was just rising. Birds were chirping in the trees around the hospital. But for Tori, it didn't feel like morning. It felt like the end of something.

"Mom?" Tori said.

"Shhh. We'll talk later," Mrs. Carsen said. She was fishing madly through her purse, looking for her car keys.

"What we have to do now is find you a doctor who knows what he's doing," Mrs. Carsen said. She was still pawing through her purse. "Darn!" she screamed. She threw her purse to the ground. "I can't find my keys."

Tori stared at her mother. Mrs. Carsen's eyes were wet with tears.

"Mom?" she said. "Mom? Are you okay?" She ran around the car and bent down to pick up her mother's purse.

"Don't cry, Mom," Tori said.

"I'm not crying," Mrs. Carsen sobbed. She pulled Tori into a tight hug. "Don't you worry, baby. I'm not crying."

Natalia jumped up off the couch as Tori and her mother walked into the living room.

"What did the doctor . . ." She stopped talking. Tori and her mother were silent and stony.

"Why don't you go rest, Tori?" Mrs. Carsen said. "I need to have a word with Roger. And then I'm going to start making some calls. It's time for us to find you a real doctor."

She disappeared into her bedroom, leaving Natalia and Tori staring after her.

Natalia turned to Tori. She shifted uncomfortably on her feet. Tori sighed and sank onto the couch. Natalia sat next to her. The girls were silent for a moment.

"He told you what Dr. Wyckoff told you, didn't he?" Natalia finally said.

Tori nodded. She felt tears come to her eyes again.

"Oh, Tori," Natalia cried. She drew Tori into her arms. "I am so, so sorry."

Tori sobbed. Natalia held her for several minutes, stroking her hair. When Tori looked up, she saw that Natalia's eyes were wet and red. She had been crying too.

"I'm so scared, Nat," Tori said. "I'm so scared."

"I know," Natalia said.

"Mom is acting like it's not true," Tori said. "But how can it not be? I have all the symptoms. Two doctors have told me I have MD."

"Maybe they're wrong," Natalia said.

Tori shook her head.

"I don't think so. Not anymore." She wiped her face with her sleeve. "I've been crying all morning. I think I'm all cried out."

"What are you going to do now?" Natalia said.

"Well, I'm not going to Disney World," Tori choked out.

Natalia stared at her, stunned.

"It's a joke," Tori said. "You know those commercials? Where they ask stars who've just won some big event—"

"I know the commercials," Natalia cut in. "I am

just surprised that you are making a joke." She paused. "Especially such a bad one!"

Now it was Tori's turn to stare.

Then she felt her mouth twitch. She started to smile. Before she knew it, she was laughing. Natalia started laughing too. Soon they were howling and clinging to each other.

"Oh, Nat," Tori finally said, gasping for breath. "This must be the worst day of my life. The worst. I've been having a lot of those lately."

"What would make you feel better?" Natalia asked.

"Being told that both doctors are full of it," Tori said. She stood up and headed for her bedroom.

"Where are you going?" Natalia asked.

"Where else?" Tori said. "I have skating practice."

Natalia's eyes widened. "You're going to continue with Nationals?"

"Of course I am," Tori said. "How can I quit now? I'll never get this chance again."

Natalia nodded.

"Well?" Tori said. "Are you coming?"

Somehow Tori made it through the day. Her heart was clutched in her chest, and her stomach was in knots. It was impossible to eat. She felt like an animal trapped in a cage.

Still, she had to muddle through. It was hard to make herself go to practice. But not going would have been even harder. It would have meant admitting that MD was getting the best of her. She wasn't ready to do that. She turned a switch in her heart to autopilot and pushed on.

Afterward she stopped by her mother's room and knocked on the door.

"Tori!" Roger's eyes were filled with worry. "We were wondering where you were. How are you doing, sweetheart?"

"I'm fine," Tori told him. "I just wanted to tell Mom I'm going down to Jill's room to hang out."

Roger glanced at Tori's skating bag. "You didn't go to practice today, did you?"

"Of course I did." Tori shifted her bag on her shoulder. "The long program is Saturday. I can't skip practice!"

Roger started to say something, but Tori walked to her room next door and began changing into a faded pair of jeans. She knew what Roger was going to say, and she had the same doubts. What if she shouldn't skate? What about the diagnosis? Shouldn't she be worrying about the future? But she pushed the thoughts from her mind. She didn't want to think about that now. She just wanted to do what felt good.

And what felt good was being around her friends.

"Hey, Tor!" Jill sang, greeting her at the door of her room. "Get in here. We just ordered hot chocolate from room service."

Tori stepped into the room and into a warm circle of friendship. Her buddies from Silver Blades were laughing and talking as always. Amber looked up, her eyes bright with expectation, and grinned happily when she saw Tori. Haley and Nikki were sprawled on the floor. Natalia was already there. She stood behind the couch. And—surprise of surprises—Veronica was there too, looking bored but sipping from a mug of hot cocoa.

"Did anyone see my practice today?" Tori asked. She walked into the room and stood in front of the TV set. "I was brilliant, as always."

"Okay, *Carla*, whatever you say," Haley teased. She tossed a handful of popcorn at Tori. "Sit down, I can't see the movie."

Jill had rented a silly, romantic movie about skating. They were watching the skating scenes and screaming with laughter at the mistakes the actors were making. Tori plopped down on the couch. She picked up a steaming mug of cocoa from the low table in front of her. She wrapped her hands around it and sipped carefully at the hot, sweet liquid.

"Ooh! Look at that! A double loop!" Haley whooped. "Don't tell me the judges are supposed to be impressed with that!"

"Did you ever see the old tapes of Peggy Fleming at the Olympics?" Nikki asked. "She lands the simplest double loop and the announcers go nuts, like she just did a triple axel!"

"Well, it was really advanced at the time," Tori pointed out. "And Peggy's form was perfect."

"Besides, she was so cute in those tapes," Jill added, giggling. "She didn't even know she was supposed to bow after her program. She just kind of skated off the ice when she was done."

"I wish we had those tapes to watch right now instead of this goofy movie," Amber complained. "Why don't we play charades?"

"Amber, you're brilliant," Haley said. She clicked off the television. "Good-bye, movie. I'll get pencils."

"I always wondered what this hotel stationery was for," Jill said, opening the drawer by the bed.

Nikki clambered over Tori and grabbed some paper from Jill. Haley and Amber declared themselves captains and began arguing about who was going to get Natalia on her team. Natalia grabbed a handful of the paper and began tearing it into long, neat strips.

Tori sighed. It felt so good to be here, with her closest friends. She set down the mug. But when she tried to let it go, she couldn't. Her fingers wouldn't uncurl from the handle.

Nobody noticed at first that Tori was rigid and silent. The mug sat on the table. Her right hand was gripped firmly around it.

Carefully, hoping not to attract attention, Tori tried to work her fingers loose. She felt as if her fingers were made of stone. The muscles squeezed tightly. They gripped the mug for dear life.

"Come on, come on," she begged, under her breath. But the harder she tried to move her fingers, the more they gripped the cup. She could see the skin of her hand growing white with the strain. She took a deep breath and tried to relax.

Why is this happening to me? she thought. Then the realization hit her: This is part of the disease. I can't let go of this mug because my muscles won't release it. It was just as Dr. Mitchell had said back at his office— she had a delayed ability to release her grip. This disease was real.

She wrestled with the cup some more, spilling some of the steaming cocoa onto her hand. Tears of frustration spilled out of her eyes and down her cheeks.

Then she realized that the room had grown quiet. She looked up. The other girls were sitting still, looking at her curiously.

"Tori," Nikki said, "are you all right?"

"No," Tori answered in a flat voice. "No, I'm not." She bowed her head and choked back tears. "I'll never be all right again."

Silence filled the room. Tori could hear the buzz of the little refrigerator in the corner.

Haley gave a nervous laugh. "Is this some kind of weird joke, Tori?" she asked.

Tori shook her head. "It's no joke."

Her cheeks felt hot with humiliation as she used her left hand to slowly peel the fingers of her right hand off the mug. She pulled her right hand into her lap and massaged it, letting her fingers relax.

"Tori, you're scaring me. What's going on?" Jill asked.

Natalia crossed the room and sat next to Tori. She took Tori's right hand in her own and began massaging it.

"It's okay," Natalia said. "You can tell them."

Tori looked up. Her friends were all gazing at her, their eyes full of fear.

"I have this disease," she finally said. "Remember when I passed out at the rink a couple of weeks ago?"

There were nods and murmurs. "Of course we remember," Haley said.

"Well, I wasn't woozy from not eating," Tori replied. "And I wasn't sleepy from having mono. I went to the doctor, and I had all these tests done. I have this thing called myotonic muscular dystrophy."

There was an awkward silence. Tori's friends looked stunned.

"Myo—mya—" Nikki struggled with the words. "What is that? What does it do to you?"

"It makes you weak," Tori said. "And stiff. And—"

"Maybe you shouldn't be out of bed," Jill said anxiously, cutting Tori off midsentence. "Let me get you a blanket."

Tori shook her head. "I don't need a blanket." She gave her friends a crooked smile. "It's a really messed-up disease. It's going to put me in a wheelchair, maybe even within a year. It's not going to kill me." She swallowed hard. "But if it's going to stop me from skating, it might as well kill me."

Natalia squeezed Tori's shoulders in a fierce hug. "I can't believe this is really happening to you, Tori."

"Are you sure those doctors got it right?" Haley asked. "You look perfectly healthy to me."

Tori smiled. "I know. I look healthy to me, too. But I need to sleep all the time, and you've seen my practices lately. It's already getting to me."

"Well, I think the doctor is crazy," Haley said decisively. "You've never let anything stand in your way. Jill, remember the story you told me about the time Tori wouldn't even admit when her appendix was bothering her?"

She turned back to Tori. "You won that local title and then went straight to the hospital." She laughed. "Tori Carsen never gives in to sickness."

"This isn't like having a bad appendix," Tori said. "It's not something you can fix. There's no cure." She looked at her hand. Now it was fine. But her body was betraying her. And there was nothing she could do about it.

Hot tears slid down Tori's cheeks, and she felt her chest heave with deep, racking sobs. Jill wrapped a blanket firmly around Tori's shoulders and pressed a tissue into her hand. Natalia leaned her head against Tori's and cried along with her. Haley stood up and began to pace.

"Do you want some popcorn?" she asked, grabbing the bowl and shoving it toward Tori. "Hey. Um. Hey, Tor, come on, it'll be okay." She patted Tori's shoulder.

Finally Tori lifted her head and swiped at the tears on her cheeks. She drew a deep, shuddering breath and then smiled weakly at her friends. "Thanks, you guys. I've been a little nuts lately. One minute I feel normal. Then I remember I have this disease and I turn into a basket case again."

"Oh, Tori, we'll do anything we can to help," Jill promised.

"Whatever we need to do to beat this thing," Haley added.

Tori grinned. And this time the smile felt real. "You guys are the best," she said.

"Yeah, yeah," Haley said, waving her hand. "Now, can we start watching the movie again? I know! Let's turn off the lights so it's like being in a movie theater." Haley's voice was louder than normal. She darted forward and pressed Play on the VCR, then dashed across the room and turned the lights off. Then she plunked back down on the couch.

"I can't stay," Amber murmured. It was the first word she'd said since Tori's announcement. She picked up her hotel room key off the table and stood up.

"Where you going, Amber?" Haley demanded. "Come on, sit down. I'm going to make more popcorn. You want more popcorn, Tori?"

Tori shook her head. Amber slipped toward the door, staying away from Tori.

"I promised my mom I'd be back early," Amber said, not meeting Tori's eyes. "I thought I mentioned it when I got here."

Amber slid out the door, pulling it shut quietly. Haley shrugged.

"She's out in space tonight," Haley said brightly. "I'll never understand Amber!"

Tori tried to concentrate on the movie. It was kind of hard to follow the plot, though. Haley kept butting in with wisecracks.

"Ha-*hem*!" Tori gave a sudden, hacking cough. A piece of popcorn had gone down the wrong way. She cleared her throat and she was fine.

"Tori! Are you all right?" Jill asked anxiously. "Let me get you some water. Or some orange juice. Vitamin C!"

"Thanks, but water's fine," Tori insisted. "I'm really okay. I can get it myself."

"Don't you dare!" Jill stood up quickly. "I was getting up anyway."

Jill crossed the room and got a glass of water. She placed it carefully on the table next to Tori. Then she hooked a bendable straw onto the glass.

"Thanks," Tori said, sipping the water.

"No problem." Jill grinned.

"Hel-lo!" Haley yelled at the screen. "Why is he wearing hockey skates for a figure-skating scene?"

Haley let out a piercing cackle. She leaned over and shoved Nikki. Nikki smiled but didn't laugh. Nobody else was joining in Haley's laughter either. The more Haley joked, the quieter everybody else became.

As soon as the credits were rolling on the movie, Jill jumped up and turned on the lights.

"Okay, everybody out," she said brightly. "Tori needs to get home. Party's over!"

"I *am* going to head out," Tori said, stretching. She was feeling sleepy. "But don't break up the party on my account!"

"Natalia, go with her," Jill said. Natalia started to get up from her seat.

Tori put a hand on Natalia's shoulder. "Sit. Stay and have fun." She looked around the room and smiled. "Guys, I'm cool! I'll see you tomorrow."

She turned toward the door, then stopped. She spun around and faced the other girls.

"There's just one more thing. Please, this has got to be our secret. If anyone finds out, I'll be done for. The judges aren't about to give out high scores to a girl who can't deliver in the Olympics. And I don't want reporters asking me questions I don't know the answers to yet. So you can't tell anyone. Not even your moms. Okay? Secret?"

"Supersecret," Jill said right away.

"Not a word," Natalia agreed.

"My mouth's on lockdown," Haley added.

Nikki nodded, and Tori smiled again.

"Thanks, you guys," she said. "Thanks for being such great friends."

Tori headed back to the suite. She let herself into the living room with her key.

As she passed her mother and Roger's room, she knocked lightly on their door. Mrs. Carsen yanked it open.

"I just wanted to say good night," Tori said.

"Darling, I need to talk to you," Mrs. Carsen said in her low voice.

"What is it?" Tori asked.

Mrs. Carsen folded her hands in a businesslike way. She thought for a moment, then spoke.

"Do you remember what Dr. Mitchell said today?" Mrs. Carsen asked.

"Every word of it, Mom. It's burned into my brain."

"About skating. Do you remember what he said about skating? He said you could hurt yourself if you skate."

Tori shrugged. "He also said he wasn't sure. He said I had to decide for myself about skating."

Mrs. Carsen sighed. "Roger tells me you went to practice today."

"Of course, Mom. What's this all about?" Tori's brow furrowed.

"Roger and I have discussed this. We called your coach, Dan, to tell him our decision. You're not going to skate in the long program Saturday."

Tori's eyes widened. "What are you saying? No!" she cried. "You can't . . ."

Mrs. Carsen arched one eyebrow and crossed her arms. Her lips were pressed together and her eyes narrowed.

"I can. And I did," she said. "We're taking you out of the competition. You're not finishing Nationals."

10

Tori felt a flash of anger. "Are you kidding me?" she shouted, gritting her teeth and curling her hands into fists. "Who do you think you are? Just—just going ahead and making a decision like this? Were you even planning on talking to me about it? Didn't you think you should *ask* me first?"

Mrs. Carsen raised her hands. "Shhh," she said, pointing to the room behind her. "Roger is sleeping."

Mrs. Carsen shut the door and led Tori over to the couch in the living room.

"Tori, sit down and listen to me. I know what I'm talking about."

"You have no *idea* what you're talking about!" Tori said loudly. "You don't know what it's like to have this stupid disease. It's like having a nightmare I can't wake up from! And you don't have the first clue about what it's like to skate at Nationals!"

Mrs. Carsen flinched.

Tori was instantly sorry. Mrs. Carsen had skated as a girl, and she had been good. But she had never made it to Tori's level. Mrs. Carsen took a deep breath.

"I know you're angry at me, but in the long run you'll agree. Skating is not worth the risk you're taking. The best thing to do right now is to concentrate on your health. I've made another appointment with a specialist in New York, at Mount Sinai Hospital. He's very good, and he'll be able to find out what's really wrong with you."

"What's *really* wrong? Mom—"

"Once you get better," Mrs. Carsen rolled on, ignoring Tori, "you can return to skating. You'll be even better! Tori, think about it logically! What if you skate with this condition, whatever it is, and you perform terribly? Then, when you do get better, the odds will be stacked against you. It'll be so much easier to just disappear from competition now and get well," she pleaded. "You can return to skating later."

"Mom, you just don't get it, do you?" Tori cried. "I *cannot* drop out now. I can't!"

"I understand how it is at your age," Mrs. Carsen said soothingly. "Every month seems like a year, and you think that you have to do it all now. But you have your whole life ahead of you! There's no rush."

"There *is* a rush!" Tori cried. "There isn't another Nationals in my future. There won't be another Olympics for me. Next year, I might not even be able to walk, let alone skate." She took a deep breath and sank back onto the couch. She looked at her mother and spoke more quietly.

"This is my dream. I'm going to skate as much as I can, and as well as I can, until I can't do it anymore!"

Tori and Natalia rushed into the locker room just before nine A.M. practice on Friday morning. Tori was late, yet she needed more sleep. She was still tired. At least she felt as if she'd survive practice.

"How are you feeling?" Natalia asked, her eyes wide with concern. She dropped Tori's practice bag onto a bench. She had insisted on carrying it.

"Super." Tori forced herself to smile. "Natalia, you didn't have to come along today. It's not like you have to practice."

"I wanted to watch." Natalia shrugged. "And I couldn't let you walk to the rink alone." Her chin trembled.

"Natalia, pull yourself together," Tori whispered. "If any reporters see you bawling, they'll know something's up."

Natalia sniffed and nodded. "Sorry," she mumbled.

Tori glanced away from Natalia. She spotted Amber and Jill changing nearby. "Hey, you guys. Where's the rest of the crew?"

"Nikki decided she'd rather go swimming in the hotel pool than watch us practice," Jill said. "Go figure. Unfrozen water."

"Where's Haley?" Tori asked.

Jill shrugged. "She's around somewhere."

Meanwhile, Amber had quietly moved her things down to the other end of the bench. She was changing with her back to Jill and Tori.

Why is Amber acting so weird? Tori wondered. "Amber, come join us. There's an empty locker right here," she said.

"That's okay," Amber mumbled, tugging on an oversized sweatshirt. "I'm done anyway." She slunk out of the locker room without another word.

"What's with her?" Tori asked.

"Never mind Amber," Jill said, pulling something out of her skate bag. "Look, I brought hot and cold packs for you." She handed two bright blue gel-filled packets to Tori. "I thought the heat would help your muscles relax. And the cold is just in case you have a fall out there," Jill explained.

"Wow, that's really sweet, Jill," Tori said. She noticed that Natalia was peering at the warm pack and sniffling again.

"It's no bother!" Jill exclaimed. "I had them anyway."

Tori sighed. "Well, thanks."

Jill was already digging in her skate bag again. "And here's a banana. It's the perfect food to keep your strength up. Did you eat breakfast?"

"I ate breakfast, Jill!" Tori said. "Anyway, I don't even like bananas!"

"Trail mix?" Jill offered.

"Jill!" Tori said. She wanted to tell her friend to act normal. But she knew Jill was just trying to help. "Come on, let's hit the ice."

Suddenly the door burst open and Haley came barreling through at top speed.

"Hold it!" she yelped. "Before you go anywhere, guess what?"

"What?" Tori asked. She wasn't in the mood for one of Haley's guessing games today.

Haley waved a business card in Tori's face. "There's a reporter out there. From *Time* magazine. She asked me to give you this. She wants an exclusive interview with you. For a feature article!"

"Hey, what about me?" Jill complained jokingly.

"Sorry, Charlie. She specifically asked to talk to Miss Tori here," Haley said, waving the card at Tori again.

Tori grabbed the business card. MARIANNE MAGNAN, REPORTER, *TIME* MAGAZINE, it read. She turned it over. Scrawled on the back was a short note: "Meet me in the coffee shop at 12:30 for lunch."

Wow, Tori thought. *Time!* This was big—not like the regular interviews she gave before and after competitions. She tried to picture what a whole article about her in *Time* magazine would look like.

"That's awesome, Tori," Jill said. "Just don't say anything dumb. And remember us when you're famous."

"Jill? Jill who?" Tori joked as they strode out of the locker room and headed for the rink. "Oh, is she one of the little people? Ah yes, the girl with the banana. I think I remember her!"

They were giggling when they got to the ice. But Tori's smile faded when she saw her coach hurrying over to her with a worried look on his face.

"Tori!" Dan said. "What are you doing here? I spoke to your mother last night. She told me what the doctor said. I thought you were dropping out of the competition."

"Dan, this is *my* decision, not my mother's," Tori explained patiently. "I'm not going to stop skating."

"But—your mom said you might have a very serious muscle condition."

"Listen." Tori grasped his hand. "Skating feels right. It feels good to me. There's no way that something that makes me feel so good could ever do me harm."

Dan sighed. "I'm not sure that's true," he said to Tori. "But you know the risk you're taking. If you want to keep skating without your mother's permission, that could be difficult. But I'll do everything I can to support you."

"That's why you're such a great coach," Tori said. "Now let's visualize some energy spheres and get out there!"

Dan nodded.

"Let me see a double toe loop, just to get started," he told her when she was warmed up.

"You got it," Tori said. She wobbled into a pathetic jump. She couldn't get the height she needed, even for this simple leap.

"Focus," Dan said in a warning tone. "Clear your mind of all distractions. You're not concentrating."

"I know," Tori admitted. She shook her head slightly, as if she could rattle the cobwebs loose. She skated in a large circle, then prepared herself for the jump. As she started to take off, she stumbled and fell.

She popped up and started skating again. She concentrated on her expression, her hand motions, and her attitude as she twirled into a layback spin. But just as her spin was at its quickest, her leg buckled. She fell to the ice. She wasn't hurt, but when she stood up, her foot twinged.

She brushed herself off and glanced up at the stands. Mrs. Carsen was nowhere to be seen.

Of course she's not here, Tori thought. She doesn't even want me to skate. I'm on my own now.

On my own.

The words echoed in her head. Concentrate on your skating! she told herself. She hitched herself into a double toe loop. In her haste, she didn't plant her feet correctly. Her blade caught in the ice. She made a pathetic hop, not even a single toe loop, then crashed down onto the ice.

She just lay there for a moment, feeling miserable. She couldn't even perform the simplest moves! She had never skated more poorly, and her mother wasn't even there to help her.

Dan was at her side in a moment. "Tori, are you sure you want to continue?" he asked, kneeling next to her.

"Of course I want to continue," Tori snapped, hauling herself to her feet. "Aren't you supposed to be telling me to get my act together? Don't treat me like a baby!"

Dan winced. Tori was instantly sorry. She was always lashing out at people lately. Dan just wanted to help.

"Sorry," she said. "Can we get back to work?"

Dan nodded.

Tori skated down the rink and moved into a series of rockers. *Forget Mom. This is about me. I've got to nail my program today,* she told herself fiercely.

She skated around the rink quickly, dancing and kicking with lively movements. She was warming up and starting to feel good. She held out her arms for balance. The fancy steps suddenly felt like flying.

Then she prepared for her double axel, a jump that would wow the judges and set the tone for the rest of her long program. When she had built up enough speed, she planted her foot and whirled into the air, snapping down to the ice with perfect precision.

She held the landing, pumping her legs in powerful back crossovers, mixing a few turns and a swirling arabesque into the routine as she worked her way across the rink. It was time for a much harder jump combination, the triple Lutz–double toe loop. It was always a challenge, but Tori had never been afraid of challenges. She planted her foot and made the triple Lutz perfectly. She felt herself whirl into the double toe loop exactly right and expected to feel the ice solidly under her again as she landed.

Just as her blade touched the ice, her leg gave out completely. A powerful muscle spasm turned her leg into a violent, searing, white-hot shot of pain.

Tori cried out and tumbled to the ice. Her leg felt like a gnarled, twisted knot.

"Tori, are you all right?" Dan cried, running to her side.

"It hurts," Tori sobbed. "Dan, it really hurts." She clenched her teeth, clutching at her leg with both hands and forcing herself to breathe deeply.

"Tori!"

She looked up to see her mother slipping and sliding across the ice. She was wearing tennis shoes and jeans, but she was determined to get to her daughter.

Tori had never been so glad to see anyone in her life.

"Mom," she called out. "Help me!"

Mrs. Carsen leaned down and grabbed Tori's hands. She pulled Tori up and grabbed her waist. The two of them walked slowly off the ice and over to the first row of seats in the arena.

Tori collapsed, then lifted her leg onto another seat. She tried to massage out the painful spasm.

"Look at my leg," she moaned. "You can actually see the muscles contracting. I can barely move my foot!"

"You need a hot pack," Dan ordered. "That's the only thing that's going to help right now."

"Jill has one," Tori informed him. "Can you get it from her?"

"I'll be back," Dan said. He left in search of Jill. Tori continued to knead the muscles in her leg. Mrs. Carsen joined in, her long fingers working at the stubborn muscle.

"I didn't know you were here," Tori said.

"I was standing where you couldn't see me," Mrs. Carsen told her. "I didn't want you to know I was watching."

"You were spying on me?"

Mrs. Carsen wrinkled her brow. "Don't be ridiculous. I just wanted to make sure you were all right."

"Well, I guess I wasn't," Tori mumbled.

Mrs. Carsen sighed. "This is precisely why I don't want you to skate your long program," she said. "You could seriously hurt yourself!"

"Mom, please. This muscle spasm is painful, but it's hardly life threatening."

"You know what I mean." Mrs. Carsen's voice was quiet but firm. "What if you have a spasm like that when you're landing after a high jump? You could land on your back or your head. Or you could crash into the boards."

"Or I could suddenly burst into flames, melt the ice, and drown," Tori said sarcastically. "I've been falling since I was five. I'm not going to hurt myself."

"This is different!" Mrs. Carsen insisted. "You're not skating the way you used to. You can't push yourself anymore. Why won't you take a rest until you get better, and then continue when the risks aren't so great?"

"Shhh!" Tori hissed. Dan would be back with the hot pack any second. The last thing she wanted was to make a scene in front of her coach, even if he did know the whole story. He would be sure to pitch in with advice, and Tori had gotten enough of that lately.

"I think Jill wins the most-prepared award," Dan announced as he returned with the warm plastic pack. "There's also a first-aid station, with more of these if you need them. Just wrap it against your leg in this towel."

"That ought to do the trick," Tori said. "Thanks, Dan. I'll be up again in no time."

"Dan, can't you talk to her?" Mrs. Carsen begged. "Tori has completely lost her mind."

Dan squatted next to Tori and looked at her leg.

"Look at her, Dan," Mrs. Carsen said. "She's not able to concentrate on her skating. She needs to focus her energy on getting well, not on skating a perfect program for a bunch of judges."

Tori swallowed hard. She *had* been focusing on skating a perfect program. But she could hardly skate at all now! And what if her mother was right? What if she only had a little energy left and was using it all up by trying so desperately to get ready for Nationals?

What if she was making herself even worse? That meant . . . She felt a wave of dizziness. That meant she would end up in a wheelchair that much sooner.

Tori's leg began to relax. The pain wasn't as bad, but she felt more hopeless. Why was her body doing this to her? She imagined what her long program would be like. She could see her leg giving out. What if she collapsed right in the middle of the program? In front of the cameras, the judges, the whole world? She tried to shove the thoughts from her mind.

"Forget Nationals," Mrs. Carsen said, hugging her hard. "Come back home with me. You can take a long rest. Then we'll decide what to do next."

Tori pushed her away. "I'm not ready to quit."

Mrs. Carsen smoothed Tori's hair. "You need to think about it."

"I've already decided," Tori said firmly. "I want to keep skating, that's my choice. And I want you to support me."

A shadow passed across Mrs. Carsen's face. "You're being completely irrational," she said. But the bossiness was gone from her voice.

"This is my last chance, Mom," Tori said. "Please."

Mrs. Carsen shook her head. But something in Tori's quiet, calm statement seemed to have moved her. "We'll see," she said.

Tori turned to Dan. "Besides, I would never quit because you two nagged me and worried until I took your advice. I would only quit if it felt right to me."

"I understand," Dan said. "Take today to think. Your mom and I are here for you."

Tori nodded and stood up. Her mother moved to help her, but she shook off her hand. "I'm fine," she insisted. "I'm going back to the hotel."

She limped to the dressing room, her leg still seizing up painfully. She dressed slowly, stopping often to reapply the hot pack. She stared at herself in the mirror.

"You look healthy," she said aloud to her reflection.

It was true. There was no hint of her illness in her face or in the strong, supple muscles of her arms and legs. The reflection didn't show what was going on inside.

Why couldn't the girl in the mirror—that "outside" healthy girl—be her?

When she was dressed, she slung her bag onto her shoulder and walked out of the rink by a side door. The walk back to the hotel was perfect exercise for her leg. She pushed down carefully on her calf with every step. She could feel the muscle respond, bit by bit.

By the time she got back to the hotel, her leg felt much better. She glanced at her watch, and suddenly her heart dipped. It was nearly twelve-thirty. Her interview! She had forgotten all about it. She hadn't even told Dan or her mother.

Tori glanced at herself in a mirror, making sure she looked all right. She did. She looked healthy, confident, and self-assured.

She hurried to the coffee shop. It was a casual but stylish spot on the ground floor of the hotel, near the lobby. The walls were white, with antique posters of cruise-line advertisements dotting the walls. There were several tables, and booths lining the walls. Tori scanned the room and spotted a young woman sitting alone. There was a small tape recorder on the table in front of her.

Tori strode up to the table, clutching her skating bag.

"Are you Marianne?" she asked.

The woman looked up and smiled. She was young

and very hip-looking, with cat's-eye glasses and a short, funky hairstyle. Tori felt more relaxed just looking at her open, friendly face.

"I sure am," the woman said. "You must be Tori!"

"The one and only," Tori said, holding her hands out with a flourish. She sat down across from Marianne. "I'm glad I had some time to talk to you today," she said, as if her schedule was booked. "I've been awfully busy, preparing for my long program and everything."

Marianne nodded sympathetically. "It must be tough," she said.

"No tougher than normal," Tori said with a carefree shrug. "Silver Blades is a tough place to learn, and my coaches aren't easy on me."

"I don't mean the training," Marianne said. She leaned closer to Tori and stretched a hand across the table. She patted Tori's hand. "How long do you have, Tori?"

Tori's forehead furrowed. "What do you mean?" she asked. "Until the long program?"

"No." Marianne shook her head. "How long before you're confined to a wheelchair?"

Tori's mouth dropped open. Who told? she thought. Who else knows about my diagnosis?

She shut her mouth and took a deep breath. She could feel her hands shaking. She quickly thrust them under the table so Marianne wouldn't see.

She forced herself to give a light laugh. "What in the world are you talking about?" she asked.

"It's all right, Tori." Marianne shook her head and looked sad. "You can tell me all about it. I found out that you've been diagnosed with a rare disease. I know you collapsed at your rink back home and had to be rushed to the doctor. I know you've been to see a doctor here, too. Why don't you just tell me the truth, so we can get the full story out there?"

13

Tori's mind raced. She knew she couldn't tell Marianne the truth. It would ruin her chances at Nationals. She would have to act calm and collected, even if she was terrified inside.

She sat back in her chair and crossed her arms. "That would be a great story . . . if it were true," she said. "I'm sorry to disappoint you, but I'm healthy as a horse."

"Oh, really?" Marianne cocked her head.

"Really." Tori laughed again. "I passed out at my rink, true. But there's no deep reason for it. I just overdid my training a little. And I guess the diet I put myself on was a little too strict."

Her heart was beating so fast, it felt like a jackhammer. But she could hear that her voice sounded convincing.

"And all those trips to the doctor—well, if you know anything about me, you know that my mother is totally protective. She freaked out and rushed me to a bunch of doctors, just to make sure nothing would affect my skating. But they all told her the same thing—I'm fine."

"But I've spoken to someone who—"

"I can't believe people are spreading these rumors!" Tori interrupted. "That's the real story. These competitions are so cutthroat! I guess there's someone out there who wants to make me look weak. Who told you all this, anyway?"

"I can't reveal my sources," Marianne said. She shook her head.

"Well, you don't have to believe me if you don't want to," Tori said. "But I can tell you, the only story here is that I've been working toward the Olympics all my life, and I'm about to make my dreams come true."

Marianne seemed to waver a little. She glanced down at her notes, then back at Tori.

"Well. Let's talk about your skating club, then. I've always heard really great things about Silver Blades. How do you like training there?"

Tori felt her insides melt with relief. She had done it! She had fooled Marianne. But she couldn't give any outward sign that she was glad the questions had finally led away from her health. She had to behave as if this whole interview were no big deal.

"Silver Blades." Tori sighed. "What can I say about

the best skating club in the country? My coach is awesome. I've learned a lot with him. Between him and my mother, I'm pushed very hard to learn to skate better. But they don't push me as hard as I push myself."

Tori kept her tone light. She went on to chat with Marianne about all sorts of stuff—the small size of Seneca Hills, the difficulty of getting into Silver Blades and staying in. She told funny stories about the other girls in Silver Blades, and she even mentioned Natalia's huge talent and how unfair it was that she couldn't skate at Nationals.

Marianne grinned as if they were two old friends chatting about their boyfriends. The two of them ordered lunch. She listened intently and asked dozens of questions about Tori's skating, her family, and her friends.

"Whoops!" Tori said as she finished off her pasta salad with fresh vegetables. "I've got to get back to the rink for my afternoon practice."

"Would you mind if I tagged along?" Marianne wanted to know. "I'd love to see you in action. I could call the photographer and have him meet us there. He could get some pictures of you skating to go with the article."

"Sure! That sounds fine," Tori said cheerfully. She hoped her mother and Dan wouldn't be too surprised if she showed up at the rink again. She was feeling better anyway. Her leg felt stronger, and it felt good to think about the interview instead of arguing about whether she should skate. It felt good to pretend everything was back to normal.

The two of them hurried back to the rink, and Tori rushed into the locker room to change.

This is the perfect example of why you always look your best for practice, she thought as she changed into a sky blue costume sprigged with dainty appliqué flowers. Just wearing the beautiful dress lifted Tori's spirits.

This reporter has to see me looking my best. And fortunately I do! thought Tori. She smiled at herself in the mirror and walked out of the locker room.

Tori saw Marianne on the other side of the lobby, chatting with Amber. She felt a sudden flash of worry. What were they talking about?

Marianne spotted Tori and waved. She said something quietly to Amber, who nodded. Then she walked toward Tori.

As Marianne walked over, Tori forced herself to put a winning smile on her face.

"I was thinking you could get a picture of me doing my illusion spins," she told her. "That would be a great action shot. But if you want to get my face in it, a simple layback would be kind of nice."

"Those sound great," Marianne said. "But the photographer will probably want candid shots, too. He's already getting his equipment ready in the rink."

"Whatever you say," Tori told her.

Tori couldn't stop thinking about what Amber and

Marianne had been talking about. But she had to put on a brave face for this reporter. No matter how much doubt she was feeling, she had to look good.

"Dan," Tori said as she and Marianne walked into the rink. "I'm just in time for my afternoon session, right?"

"Tori?" Dan looked confused. "I thought you were going to—"

"Be here early? I know, I'm sorry if I'm late," Tori interrupted. "Have you met Marianne? She's a reporter for *Time*."

Dan looked at Tori, then at Marianne. For a second, Tori was afraid he was going to mention Tori's awful morning. But he just smiled and shook Marianne's hand.

Tori stretched and took a few turns around the rink. The interview had given her a rush of adrenaline, and she was feeling good. The cramp in her leg was totally gone. She did a few practice jumps and landed them solidly.

"Dan, I'm ready," she called out. "Should I run through my long program?"

Dan nodded, and Tori launched into her opening move. Her music was upbeat and energizing. Even though it wasn't playing, Tori tried to match her movements to the rhythm of the music in her head. Her first jump, the double axel, went well—she hit it just right. Then she stroked around the rink a little more, going through the fancy footwork of her choreography.

Her spins were tight, and her arabesque was expertly done. The only problem was her spirit. Tori could feel that she was technically doing fine. But she wasn't feeling quite up to performing. She wasn't excited or sure of herself. Every move was perfect, but uninspired.

Still, it was just what a reporter needed to see. Especially a reporter with a photographer along. Tori made sure there were lots of long pauses that would make good photo opportunities. She just hoped Marianne and the photographer knew what they were.

At the end of her long program, there was a flying camel that was supposed to be easy. She had completed the move a million times—that was why it was at the end of her program, when she would be tired. She let her mind wander for a moment. That threw her off, and she wobbled slightly on the landing.

"Whoops!" she said, and bent over to stop herself from falling. Her hand barely brushed the ice for a second; then she popped right back up. She gave Dan a rueful smile, shrugged, and lifted her arms with a triumphant flourish.

Breathing heavily, she held her finishing pose for a moment, then brought her arms down and skated to Dan.

"What did you think? Not bad, right?" she asked.

Dan nodded politely. "We can go over the fine points by ourselves."

"I can take a hint," Marianne said brightly. She grinned at Tori. "What a great skater you are," she gushed. "Thank you so much for letting me sit in on this. I really feel like I've seen a champion in action!"

"Wow! Thanks," Tori said, smiling.

Inside, though, she was unhappy with her performance. It was great that Marianne liked it. But if Tori skated like that in front of the judges, she would be in serious trouble. There was no emotional drive in her program, and that stupid mistake would cost her, even if she nailed all the more difficult jumps.

The fact was, right now she wasn't skating well enough to win a medal.

Tori was up against Carla Benson, as well as Jill and Amber from Silver Blades. Then there were Fiona Bartlet and Tracy Wilkins. Tori had seen them all skate, and she knew she wasn't up to their level right now. If any one of them skated her best, she would beat Tori hands down.

Should I really go through with this? Tori wondered. Maybe I should just let Marianne get the big scoop: Tori Carsen is going to quit while she's ahead.

"When you win the Olympic gold, I'm going to look back at this article and say, 'I knew her when . . . ,'" Marianne went on. "Will you let me interview you again when you're a big Olympic star?"

Tori could hardly believe it. Marianne really did think she was good! The black cloud of doubt lifted, and she found herself giving Marianne a real smile.

"You bet," she said. "In fact, you can count on it."

"Well, I'd better motor if I'm going to get this story written by deadline," Marianne said. "They left a spot open in the magazine just for this piece, Tori. The magazine prints tonight and it will be on newsstands tomorrow."

"I can't wait to see it!" Tori said.

"Thanks for everything, Tori!"

Tori watched Marianne leave the rink. She sighed. It had taken every ounce of her strength to act normal. And it had worked! The reporter was convinced that Tori was healthy and ready to skate at Nationals.

Now all Tori had to do was fool the judges.

The Taste of Heaven banquet room at the hotel was decorated with tinsel ice skates that hung from each chandelier. Each table had a flowery centerpiece, and the tablecloths were white linen. The room looked as if a wedding banquet had been scheduled for that evening.

But it wasn't a wedding. It was a private dinner for all the skaters at Nationals and their families and friends.

Tori and Natalia were the first skaters from Silver Blades to arrive. Tori let her mother and Roger get their own table, and the three girls—Tori, Natalia, and Veronica—picked a table for themselves.

"How about this one?" Natalia asked. "We can be in the back, and nobody will bother us."

"Are you kidding?" Tori went straight for a table in

the middle of the room. "This is where the Silver Blades should be sitting. Right in the middle of all the action."

In spite of how happy she was acting, Tori was feeling lousy inside. The warm glow of her interview had worn off. She had stolen a couple of hours of sleep after her afternoon practice, but she still felt exhausted. The emotions of that morning had robbed her of a lot of strength. And the old doubts had returned. She could skate for a reporter. But could she skate for a panel of judges? She wasn't sure.

Still, she wanted to look as if she were in control. She carefully imitated the old, confident Tori. The old Tori would want to be the center of attention.

"All right," Natalia said doubtfully. She leaned in close to Tori. "Are you sure you're all right?"

"I'm fine, Natalia!" Tori said. "Look, there's Haley."

Haley made a beeline for Tori's table. "Hi, guys," she said, sitting down.

Jill and Nikki arrived next and plunked into their chairs. Tori saw Jill's parents join Roger and Corinne at the grown-ups' table.

There were two seats left at the table.

"Where's Amber?" Tori asked.

"There she is," Haley said. "Yo, Amber!" she yelled, waving at the door. "Come on, quick, before someone takes your seat!"

Amber was walking in with her mother. She glanced at Haley. Amber's mother quickly put a hand on her arm. She leaned down and whispered in her ear. Amber nodded. Then she made her way over to the Silver Blades' table.

"Sit here, Amber," Tori said, patting the empty chair next to her. She wanted to ask Amber what she and Marianne, the reporter, had been talking about.

"Um, that's okay," Amber said. She took the other empty chair, between Nikki and Jill. "This seat is fine."

Tori peered at Amber.

"Tori, will you pass the butter, please?" Jill said. Tori pushed the butter plate toward Nikki. Nikki held it out for Amber to pass to Jill.

Instead of taking the butter dish, Amber kept her hands at her sides. Her face looked pale and tense.

"Amber!" Nikki said. "Would you pass this to Jill, please?"

Amber glanced nervously in Tori's direction and then at the dish. She still didn't take it. Jill finally reached across Amber and grabbed the butter dish from Nikki.

"Earth to Amber!" Jill said. "Why didn't you hand me the butter?"

Amber glanced at Tori again.

Tori stared back. Should she ask Amber what was wrong? Before she could say a word, Carla Benson appeared in the doorway and walked over to the Silver Blades table.

"Hell-lo, ladies," Carla said in a sickly sweet voice. She lowered herself into the last empty chair and fluffed up the flounces of her dress. "Doesn't this banquet room look pretty tonight?"

Everyone at the table shut up. They all stared at Carla. Why was she sitting at their table?

"Yeah, it looks okay," Jill finally said with false politeness.

"It reminds me of the sweet sixteen party my parents just threw for me. Over two hundred people came." Carla gave an embarrassed little shrug. "Sorry I couldn't invite all of you!"

Haley snorted loudly.

"A-hem," she said, glancing Carla's way. "That piece of bread went down the wrong way."

If Carla knew Haley was being sarcastic, she ignored her.

"So, Jill, will Mrs. Carsen be designing skating outfits for *you* now?"

Jill looked confused. "Mrs. Carsen? She only designs Tori's skating outfits," she pointed out.

"Oh, I know, but I thought now that . . ." Carla stopped suddenly and pursed her lips. "Well, you know."

"We don't know," Tori said. "Why don't you tell us?"

Carla looked around, then leaned across the table confidentially.

"Oh, Tori. You don't have to pretend with me," she said. A sympathetic smile spread slowly across her face. "We're your friends! And I, for one, am *so* sorry that you have to drop out of the competition."

Tori gasped. She couldn't believe it! How did Carla know about her disease? Who else knew? She remembered the act she had put on for Marianne that morning. How many more times would she have to fake it like that in front of people?

"I don't know where you're getting your information, Carla," Tori said in an equally sweet tone. "I appreciate your concern, but I'm not dropping out of Nationals."

"Oh! That's not what I heard!" Carla shrugged.

"Well, you heard wrong," Tori said coldly. "If you're trying to psych me out, you're barking up the wrong tree."

A waiter put a basket of bread on the table. Tori picked up a roll and spread some butter on it. "I'm surprised you would resort to such cheap tactics," she added.

"Psych you out? Why would I do that?" Carla asked. She drummed her fingers on the table. "I'm just being friendly. I mean, it sounds like a pretty nasty case that you have."

Carla reached for the bread basket and took out a roll. She began spreading butter on it.

"Ooh, Carla!" Haley grimaced. "Are you sure you should be having butter? I thought you were having . . . well, you know, *trouble* with your weight."

Carla's butter knife halted in midair. She glared at Haley.

Thanks, Haley, Tori thought, grateful that her friend had made Carla drop the subject.

Carla placed her bread on her plate. She shrugged and turned back to Tori.

"I'm no doctor," she said. "And of course I never get sick. My skating is too important to me. I just wouldn't allow myself to become unhealthy."

Tori sighed. Carla wasn't going to drop the subject.

"Someone said you have some kind of flu," Carla went on. "Or maybe . . . mononucleosis."

Tori let out a long sigh of relief. Carla didn't know anything! She was just fishing around, hoping to get Tori to talk.

"So, Tori," Carla said as she sipped the soup the waiter had just placed before her. "Did you twist your ankle during practice this morning?"

"No," Tori said.

"That's funny. I heard you were limping back from the hotel after your morning practice. Maybe you should take it easy," Carla said.

"Oh, yes," Tori answered, as if she were just remembering. "I did have a little soreness after practice this morning. I guess I didn't cool down enough when I was done skating. . . . After all, I had to rush to meet with a reporter from *Time* back at the hotel."

"A reporter?" Carla asked. She shot Tori a withering glare. "She probably just wanted to find out what's wrong with you," she said. "We all know something's up."

Tori felt her teeth grind together. She forced herself to sip her soup.

"Carla, don't you have friends you can sit with?" Haley asked loudly.

A few skaters at the surrounding tables glanced over.

Tori blushed. Why had she chosen this stupid table in the middle of the room? People were starting to stare. Suddenly her appetite was gone.

"I'm not so hungry," she said. "I think I might cut out of here before they serve the main course."

Before her friends could protest, Tori took her napkin off her lap, dropped it onto the table, and stood up.

And felt her leg collapse under her.

She caught herself immediately with a hand on the table. Her leg was all right. It was just a momentary weakness. And really, stumbling when you get up from a table is no big deal, she thought.

Unless you've been diagnosed with a disease.

A disease that will cause you to lose all muscle control.

"My foot fell asleep," Tori said. She made herself smile. "That's such a gross feeling."

Carla stared at her but didn't say anything.

Tori gritted her teeth as she left the banquet room. Carla had ruined her whole night. Between keeping up appearances for her worried friends and battling Carla, Tori was exhausted.

"Tori, wait up!" Jill caught up with her friend just as she was leaving. "Can you get back to your room okay?"

Tori sighed. "Yes, I can," she said impatiently. "Of

course I can! Here come my mom and Roger and Natalia and Veronica. What could possibly go wrong?"

"Sorry," Jill said. "Look, let's get up early and get our hands on *Time* magazine, huh? Say, six-thirty tomorrow?"

Tori smiled. "That would be great!"

"I'll come by first thing," Jill said, squeezing Tori's shoulder. "See you then!"

Tori nodded and yawned. She was exhausted. So tonight was a total wash. Tomorrow would be better. She had a national magazine story all about herself to look forward to.

It seemed as if Tori had just gotten into bed when she had to reach out and turn off her alarm.

"No," she groaned, switching it off. She peeked at the time. Six A.M.? Why in the world . . .

Then she remembered. The magazine article! Suddenly Tori was wide awake. She whisked herself out of bed and hopped into a pair of jeans. When she ran out the door, Jill was already waiting for her.

"I've got the money," she said, holding up some dollar bills. "Let's get *Time*!"

The two girls rushed down to the lobby. The magazine was stuffed in a rack next to the gift shop. They dropped their money onto the counter and grabbed the top copy.

Jill whipped open the magazine and started thumbing through the pages. Tori's heart was beating like a jackhammer.

"Come on, where is . . . aha!" Jill shouted. She suddenly became pale. The smile vanished from her face. Her eyes widened.

"What is it?" Tori asked. "What's wrong?"

Jill didn't answer. Tori grabbed the magazine from her. The first thing she saw was the picture: Tori with a hand on the ice, bent over awkwardly, her legs flying and her face contorted with confusion and fear.

Then she saw the headline:

Can This Skater Go On?

Muscle Disease May Cut Short Tori's Career!

15

"Oh, no!" Tori cried. She sank helplessly onto a couch in the lobby, her hands crumpling the magazine.

"How could this happen? Who could have told?" she cried.

Jill sat next to her. They both read the entire article in horrified silence. Marianne seemed to know everything: the diagnosis, Tori's visits to the doctors, every instance of weakness in the past month. She had really done her job.

And now she was ruining Tori's life.

"How did she find out?" Tori said, pushing the hair away from her tear-stained face. "I asked you guys not to tell. I asked you all . . ."

Suddenly Tori remembered that Amber *hadn't* been in the room when Tori asked her friends to keep her MD a secret. So what had Amber been telling that reporter in the lobby of the ice arena yesterday?

Tori started thinking about how Amber had been avoiding her, too. And the way she had refused to touch the butter plate Tori had passed at the banquet.

Tori closed the magazine and stood up.

"Come on," she said. "There's someone I have to talk to."

Jill followed Tori into the elevator and up to the third floor. Tori rushed down the hall to Suite 306, Amber and her mother's suite. It was still barely light outside, but Tori pounded on the door anyway.

"What is it? Wait a minute," Amber's voice said sleepily. The door opened.

When Amber saw Tori, her eyes widened and she took three steps backward.

"What's the matter, Amber?" Tori said accusingly. "Is your conscience bothering you?"

"What are you talking about?" Amber asked in a panicky voice. She kept backing up and fell into a chair that was behind her. "Tori, why are you so mad?"

" 'Tori, why are you so mad?' " Tori mimicked. Her eyes were thin, angry slits. She leaned all the way forward and shook the magazine in Amber's face.

"You know perfectly well why I'm mad," she shouted. "You talked to that reporter about my illness."

"What is that?" Amber grabbed the magazine and looked at the article. "Oh, no. Tori, it's about you!"

Tori gave an exasperated sigh. "Of course it's about me! Did you think I wouldn't notice that you were talking to Marianne yesterday? Why did you do it, Amber? Was it to get me out of the competition? Did you think you'd somehow become national champion if I was out of the way?"

"I didn't tell her anything, Tori. I promise!" Amber said.

Something in Amber's shocked tone told Tori she was telling the truth. But Tori was still furious. She couldn't stop yelling.

"If you didn't tell, then who did?" Tori wanted to know. "You've been avoiding me like the plague. You wouldn't even sit next to me last night. You obviously have something to hide!"

"No, that's not true!" Amber insisted. "I don't have anything to hide. I'm just scared! I don't want to catch whatever it is you have."

Suddenly Tori felt tired. She looked into Amber's eyes for a long moment. Amber was telling the truth. She *was* scared. But she wasn't mean.

"Amber, you can't catch muscular dystrophy," Tori said gently. "It isn't contagious."

Amber sniffled and nodded.

Tori studied Amber. She looked incredibly young and small, sitting in the chair in her pajamas, biting her lip. Amber looked up. Her chin wobbled.

"I'm really sorry I've been staying away from you," Amber said. Her voice caught, and she gave a little sob. "I didn't mean to make you feel bad. I just got so scared!"

Tori hugged her friend, letting the younger girl cry in her arms.

"I'm scared too," Tori admitted. She looked up at Jill, who was standing uncomfortably by the door.

Tori's eyes fell on the magazine. She had dropped it on the floor. It had fallen open to the awful picture and the awful headline about her.

"If you didn't tell anyone, then who could have told?" Tori asked.

Amber sighed. "I think—I think it was my mother. She was talking to that reporter. I guess my mom didn't realize it was such a big secret."

Tori gave a frustrated sigh. How could anyone not know? But she realized that people couldn't understand something like this unless they had gone through it themselves.

"I know you're upset, Tor," Jill said. She stooped over and picked up the magazine. "But you know, the article is kind of nice. It's all about your courage. The way you're continuing to skate even with this disease."

Courage? Tori shook her head. She wasn't courageous. She was terrified. And now *Time* magazine had probably just wiped out any chance of her ever skating in a competition again.

The room was silent. Amber sniffled a little and hugged Tori tighter. Jill came over and held Tori's hand for a moment.

After a little while, Tori said good-bye to Amber and left the room. She needed to be alone. She rode the elevator to her own floor. She could hear the people in the hotel beginning to stir all around her.

Tori unlocked the door to the living room suite. Her mother was sitting on the couch. Her nose was red and her eyes were shiny. Tori looked down and saw a box of Kleenex and a copy of *Time*.

"Tori!" Mrs. Carsen said, looking up. She quickly wiped at her eyes. "You didn't tell me you spoke to this reporter."

"I know," Tori said numbly. "I forgot. I'm going to my room now."

As Tori started walking toward the room, her mother let out a sob.

"How could they do this?" she asked, clutching her bathrobe.

"You should be happy," Tori said. "Now you get what you want."

"What do you mean?" Mrs. Carsen asked.

"I've decided not to skate," Tori answered in a flat voice. "For me, the competition is over."

16

Tori lay facedown on her bed in her hotel room, sobbing. She kept trying to imagine what her life would be like without skating.

The cool air of the rink. Breaking in a new pair of skates. The frustration of trying to learn a new jump. The joy of finally landing it.

She loved waking up at dawn and driving through Seneca Hills while the town was still asleep. She loved watching the sunrise before practice. She did her homework to the hum of a car or a city bus. Most of all, she had the best friends in the world—friends who loved skating as much as she did. All this was coming to an end.

She wanted to talk to her friend Danielle Panati. Dani had been a member of Silver Blades. And she had chosen to walk away from skating to concentrate on school. She would know how much it hurt to stop.

There was one big difference, though. Dani had decided for herself to stop skating. Tori hadn't chosen muscular dystrophy. It had chosen her. And now it would rob her of nearly everything she loved.

"Hey, mopey."

The voice cut into her thoughts sharply. She looked up. Veronica was standing at the door.

"Veronica, could you please go away?" Tori sniffled. "I'm trying to think."

"You have to be facedown on a sopping wet pillow to think?" Veronica asked.

Tori sighed. "What do you want?" she asked. Veronica sat on the other bed and pulled her legs under her.

"I don't know," she said. "I feel bad. Do you want me to do anything?"

Tori sat up in bed, clutching the pillow to her chest. Suddenly anger flowed through her in a red-hot wave.

"No! I don't want you to do anything. I don't want anyone to do anything! I just want my friends, and all those reporters, and Mom and Roger and you to leave me *alone!*"

Tears streamed down Tori's face.

Veronica crossed the room and sat next to Tori. She put an arm around Tori's quivering shoulders.

"We can't leave you alone," Veronica finally said. "We're all really worried about you. Roger, and your mom, and Natalia, and Evan—"

"Evan?" Tori cried. "You told Evan about my disease?" Who doesn't know about it by now? she wondered. It seemed as if the whole world knew.

"I'm sorry, Tori," Veronica said. "That's what I mean. Nobody knows what they're supposed to do, or how they're supposed to act."

Tori sighed. "You're the only one who's been acting normal through this whole thing," she said.

"Well, I always thought you were a weird little priss who was obsessed with skating," Veronica said, smiling. "And whether you skate or not, you'll always be a weird little priss to me."

Tori wiped her cheeks and looked at Veronica. A smile spread across her face. Tori started laughing. Veronica started laughing too. But she didn't let go of Tori.

"Wow, that's better," Veronica said. "You look scary when you cry."

"Thanks." Tori sniffled again. "You look scary even when you're not crying."

"Ha, ha. Sounds like you're feeling better." Veronica gave Tori's shoulders a final squeeze and stood up. "Come on. I'll walk you down to the rink."

The rink. It was time for Tori to tell her coach that she was dropping out of Nationals.

Tori went into the bathroom and washed her face with cool water. Veronica's powder compact was on the sink. She dabbed some powder on her red nose and combed her hair.

She wanted to act brave when she told Dan and her

friends that she had decided not to skate. It would help to look as if she hadn't been crying.

Tori dressed in a pair of jeans and a long-sleeved black bodysuit. She accented the simple outfit with a beaded necklace, pulled her hair into a low ponytail, and checked herself out in the mirror. She looked poised. And her eyes were hardly puffy at all.

"Ready to face the world?" Veronica asked when Tori walked out of the bathroom.

"I think so," Tori said. "Ready to face the world with my big announcement."

Half an hour later, Tori stood outside the locker room at the rink. She could hear laughter and chatter inside. Other skaters were getting ready for practice.

She was glad she had decided to come. Although it was going to be hard to be in the locker room after the decision she had just made, she really needed to be around her friends.

As soon as she walked in, the chatter stopped. Jill, Haley, Nikki, Amber, and Natalia were all there. Instead of greeting her, they stared at her, startled. It was as if they had been caught doing something wrong.

"Hey, guys," Tori said.

She spotted a copy of *Time* magazine on a bench and waved her hand at it. "I take it you all saw the article?"

Jill snatched up the magazine and crumpled it into a ball. She stuffed it into a trash can and walked over to Tori.

"Forget about that," she said. "Don't even think about it! Sit, sit." Jill shoved a pile of Nikki's clothes onto the floor. Nikki started to object, but Jill shot her a warning look.

"I don't need to sit down," Tori insisted. She walked closer to the bench. "So what are you guys—"

"What a waste of paper," Haley cut in. She snorted. "Can you believe they killed trees just to make the paper that trash was printed on?"

Tori picked up Nikki's clothes and piled them back on the bench.

"Well, I guess—oops! Sorry, Amber," Tori said. Amber was standing behind Tori, and Tori had stepped on her foot.

Tori walked over to the lockers and leaned on them. Amber slowly moved next to Tori and leaned against the lockers too, almost touching Tori. She looked up at Tori with sad eyes.

"Natalia, are you okay?" Tori asked. The Russian skater had her hands over her eyes. She looked as if she were about to cry.

"Oh . . . oh, Tori!" Natalia wailed. She jumped up and rushed to Tori. She threw her arms around Tori's neck and burst into deep, racking sobs.

"Oh, boy," Tori muttered. This wasn't making her feel better. It was making her feel worse!

"Natalia, get off of her!" Jill tugged at Natalia's arm. "You're going to make her fall down!"

Natalia backed up suddenly, clapping her hands over her mouth.

"Oh, Tori, I'm so sorry," she said. She began crying again.

"It's okay, Nat. I'm fine," Tori said. "I wish you guys would—Amber!"

Amber was standing practically nose-to-nose with Tori.

"Why are you standing so close to me?" Tori asked.

"I wanted you to know that I know you're not contagious," Amber announced. "I'm not afraid of catching anything." She raised her chin proudly.

Tori burst out laughing. She sank helplessly onto the bench, laughing until tears streamed down her face.

"Are you all right?" Jill asked.

"I think she's hysterical," Haley said.

That made Tori laugh harder. As she stared at her friends, the tears of laughter melted into tears of frustration.

Her friends crowded around her, letting her cry. When she was done, she felt a lot better.

"Tori, why were you laughing?" Amber finally asked.

"You guys. All of you." Tori shook her head and wiped her face with the tissue Jill handed her. "Look at how you've been acting. Natalia, I know you're sad that I'm sick. But when you get weepy, it just reminds me that there's something to be sad about."

Natalia nodded gravely. She forced herself to smile.

"And Haley," Tori said, "you're the opposite. You make everything into a joke."

"I just wanted to make you feel better," Haley said quietly.

"That's awesome," Tori told her. "But sometimes I'm still going to be sad. I'd be crazy if I wasn't sad sometimes.

"And Jill!" she continued. "You take great care of me, but I've got a mom. And believe me, one mom is enough."

"But the other day—" Jill said.

"The hot pack came in really handy," Tori interrupted. "But I would have survived without it."

Tori looked around at her girlfriends.

"People like reporters and judges and complete strangers will look at me now and think, Hey, there's the skater with the muscle disease." Tori sighed.

"You guys have known me forever," she continued. "You're the ones who know the real me. So you're the only ones who can treat me like *me*."

Tori's friends nodded.

"We will, Tori," Amber said. "You can count on us."

Tori sighed.

"I have to tell you something else," she said. "I'm not going to compete tomorrow. I'm not skating my long program. I'm dropping out of Nationals." Tori's voice cracked. She sat still, forcing back her tears. She gulped and continued talking.

"I'm never skating competitively again. I need your support more than ever. Not your pity, or your sorrow, or your fear, or even your jokes. I just need your friendship. Treat me the way you always have. Because if you don't . . ."

Tori's voice trembled a bit.

". . . because if you don't," she whispered, "who will?"

I'm getting sick of this hotel room, Tori thought. She was lying on the bed, watching a boring soap opera. She didn't know where else to go. If she went out, she might run into a reporter or a pitying well-wisher. She didn't want to talk to anyone.

She sat up in bed and bent all the way forward, stretching her legs. She grasped the bottoms of her feet and flexed them. She stretched her inner thigh muscles. Then she straddled into a split. The stretches felt good. Her muscles were supple and limber today. How long did she have before they turned to stone forever?

She relaxed her muscles and sat up. There was a knock at the door.

"Who is it?" she called out.

"It's Mom," Mrs. Carsen answered.

"Come in," Tori called.

The door opened and Mrs. Carsen walked in. She was wearing designer jeans, a linen shirt, and a simple hair clip.

"I'm surprised you let me in," she admitted. "I thought I'd be the last person you'd want around."

"Why?" Tori shrugged. "You were right. I have no business skating. It just took me a while to realize it."

Mrs. Carsen sat on the bed next to Tori and put a cool hand on her arm. "I know I put a lot of pressure on you to stop skating."

"You gave me a direct order," Tori said. Which I didn't follow, she added to herself.

Mrs. Carsen sighed. "I guess I was a bit . . . forceful. But only because I'm concerned about your health," she said. "The worst thing about this disease is that it's out of your control. And I tried to take more control away from you by forbidding you to skate. That was wrong, Tori. And I apologize."

Tori was speechless. She wrinkled her forehead. Her mother was apologizing?

"Roger and I have been talking about this. And Veronica put in her two cents. I realize something now. I was wrong to impose my wishes on you. Especially now, when you have such a big decision to make." Mrs. Carsen squeezed Tori's hands and looked deep into her eyes.

"You've grown into a wonderful, smart, sensible young woman," Mrs. Carsen continued. "I have to trust you to make this decision on your own—to skate or not to skate. And whatever you decide, I'm behind you. One hundred percent."

"But Mom, I've already decided—"

"Shhh." Mrs. Carsen kissed Tori's forehead. "There's one more thing I want you to know. I've had a terrible time accepting your illness."

Oh, no, Tori thought. Is she going to make me see a third doctor? But Mrs. Carsen surprised Tori again.

"I've had a terrible time," she repeated. "But not because I'm ashamed to have a daughter with a disability. It's because I can't stand watching your dreams get taken away. Even more than that, it's because I can't stand to see you suffer in any way. Someday, when you have children of your own, you'll understand what I'm talking about. A mother loves her child fiercely, Tori. I will always love you. I will always be proud of you. Always. No matter what."

"Oh, Mom!" Tori hadn't realized how badly she needed to hear that. She hugged her mother. Tears stung her eyes for the third time that day.

"I love you too, Mom," she said, resting her forehead against her mother's. They laced their fingers together. "The truth is, I was almost relieved when you told me I couldn't skate. That meant I didn't have to make the decision myself."

Mrs. Carsen opened her mouth to speak, but she was interrupted by another knock on the door.

"Yes?" she said.

The door opened a crack. Jill popped her head in. "Mrs. Carsen, is it okay if we come in?"

Mrs. Carsen looked at Tori, who nodded.

"I'll give you and your friends some privacy," Mrs.

Carsen said. She walked out the door. Jill poked her head through. "Hi!" she said.

"Don't tell me," Tori said. "You've brought me a portable heart-and-lung machine."

Jill grimaced and smiled. "No, I'm not going to be Dr. Jill anymore," she said. She came into the room and sat on the other twin bed. Amber, Natalia, Haley, and Nikki were with her—and Veronica.

"We brought you this," Haley said, holding out an oversized homemade card. "It's from all of us."

Tori recognized the drawing on the card as a Haley Arthur special. It was Tori's name, decorated with skates, flowers, and goofy smiley faces. Inside was a message in big, bold letters: YOU'LL ALWAYS BE OUR CHAMPION.

Everyone had signed it, with hearts. Tori could almost feel their love and support coming off the page. She beamed at her friends.

"Thank you so much, you guys," she said. "I'm sorry I sort of flipped out before."

"Hey, you didn't flip out," Haley said. "And even if you did, we would have deserved it. We've been acting like weirdos."

Tori shook her head. "I've been the weirdo," she said. "I just don't know . . . I don't know what to do."

"I knew it," Jill said. "I knew you didn't really want to give up competing."

Tori looked up. "I don't want to," she said. "But I have to."

Veronica stepped forward and joined the other girls on the twin bed across from Tori's.

"Says who? You're not in a wheelchair yet. I think you should go for it," she said.

"You're always telling me to get a life outside the rink," Tori said. "Why do you care if I skate?"

"I *didn't* care at first," Veronica said, shrugging. "But only because I never had anything as important to me as skating is to you. I didn't get it. Now that I know you better and I've seen you skate, I get it. When you skate, you're on top of the world."

Veronica ran a hand through her auburn hair and leaned toward Tori. "You've got to skate until you can't skate anymore," she declared. "Otherwise you'll always wonder what might have been."

"What's the worst-case scenario?" Haley piped up. "So you fall on your butt. No one's going to laugh at you or look down on you. They'll know you had the guts to go for it, against all the odds."

"But if you quit now," Nikki added, "they'll think you've been beaten by the disease."

"Wait, you guys," Amber said, holding her hands. "We all want Tori to skate. But skating is Tori's decision. Why should she compete if she doesn't want to? What would be the point of that?"

Tori took a deep breath. Amber was right. It would be stupid to step onto the ice in front of thousands of people if she didn't want to skate.

But Tori knew suddenly that she did want to skate. She had never stopped wanting to skate in Nationals.

She had been afraid—afraid she would fall, afraid everyone would judge her, afraid she would let down her friends and family and herself.

She stared at Natalia, Veronica, Jill, Haley, Nikki, and Amber. They all stared back. Waiting.

Tori bit her lower lip.

"You guys know me so well. Better than anyone else on the planet." Her blue eyes burned brightly.

"I'm not afraid to skate anymore," Tori declared. "I'm nervous, but that's different. I've wanted to skate in Nationals since I was eight years old. I'm going to do it. And I'm not just going to try. I'm going to *win*."

17

"Would the last group of ladies singles skaters please take the ice for a five-minute practice? The last group of ladies. Please take the ice for your practice," the announcer's voice boomed over the loudspeakers in the packed arena. A Zamboni machine rolled over the last patch of scruffy ice and crawled off the rink.

Tori tugged down on her red skating dress. She walked past a row of television cameras to the opening in the boards. She slipped off her skate guards and stepped onto the glassy ice.

It was just about time for her to skate her long program. She was in the last group of skaters, along with Carla, Amber, Jill, Tracy Wilkins, and Fiona Bartlet.

Tori had to warm up her muscles and then wait until it was her turn to skate. She circled the rink, breathing deeply and trying to loosen up.

She felt awful. She had gone to sleep at nine o'clock the night before and had slept like a stone for twelve hours. But all the emotional strain of the past few days had robbed her of strength.

Fatigue made her bones ache. She felt as if gravity were dragging her down. The insides of her elbows, the backs of her knees, and the pit of her stomach all felt like lead.

She picked up speed and skated quickly around the rink again. She had stretched carefully, and she felt as if her muscles were warmed up. There weren't any sudden spasms or painful knots.

She tried to ignore the din of conversation from the spectators jammed into the arena. She lifted her left leg into a spiral, forcing it to go higher even though her leg felt like a plank of wood.

She brought her leg down and moved into backward crossovers. Then she launched herself into a simple double toe loop. She wobbled on the landing. She gritted her teeth and tried again. This time she almost fell. She heard a group of teenagers in the front row gasp as she righted herself.

What in the world am I doing out here? she thought frantically. What made me think I could skate?

She felt panic take over her body.

"Ahem." Someone coughed nearby. Tori looked over just in time to see Carla Benson execute a perfect triple toe loop. Carla skated in a small circle around Tori, smirking at her as she pretended to adjust the strap on her costume.

Tori smiled back. Carla's eyebrows went up and she skated away.

Thanks, Carla! Tori thought. That was all I needed to get me going. Now I feel great. And beating you is going to feel even better!

Adrenaline rushed through Tori's body, spreading a warm glow through her arms and legs. She skated across the rink and whipped herself into a perfect sit spin. She crossed the rink again and leaped into a graceful triple toe loop.

"Please clear the ice! Please clear the ice!" the announcer's voice rang out. The five-minute practice was over.

Tori passed the cameras and walked out of the arena. She found a quiet spot in the hall outside to wait her turn. Dan and Mrs. Carsen followed her.

"Nice practice, Tori," Dan said. "You really looked strong near the end there. How do you feel?"

"Not bad," Tori said. She didn't want to jinx the confidence that had started to flow through her after Carla's attempt to upset her.

"You're skating last, so you've got to keep your muscles warm, sweetheart," Mrs. Carsen said. She wrapped a flannel towel over Tori's legs and rubbed them vigorously.

Tori heard the crowd cheer as the first competitor took the ice. She tried to block out the noise, but with each program, the crowd grew more and more enthusiastic.

The familiar music from Jill's program floated backstage. Tori tried to ignore the lyrical, beautiful music. It was an Andrew Lloyd Webber composition called "You Must Love Me." She couldn't block out the music. She had seen Jill skate to the song at practice all week. She knew Jill's routine by heart.

The music came to a dramatic peak. Tori heard the crowd groan. She knew Jill must have missed an important jump. The applause at the end of Jill's routine was long and loud.

Tori felt bad for Jill. No matter what, she always wanted her friends to skate well.

She knew from the music that Carla Benson was next.

She looked over at Dan. He was staring back at her. He walked over to her.

"Think about your routine, Tori," he said. "*Your* routine. Not Carla's."

She nodded. She walked over to a full-length mirror in the hall and studied herself. Her dress was a deep red velvet that her mother had designed.

When Tori had first seen it, she'd had to struggle not to show how much she hated it. It was the first dress her mother had ever made that she couldn't stand. She thought it made her look pale. And it made her waist look fat!

But now, as she studied it again, she noticed that the red color made her blond hair glow.

And it didn't make her waist look thick. Not at all. It was cut to hug her slender, tall body.

Suddenly she realized that the dress was lovely. It

had been her anger at her mother that had clouded her vision before.

Mrs. Carsen walked up behind her and put her hands on her shoulders. She looked into the mirror at her daughter.

"You look beautiful, baby," she whispered.

Tori reached up and put her hands over her mother's.

"Thanks, Mom. For the dress. For everything."

She turned around and snuggled against her mother.

"I'm scared, Mom," she said.

"Shhh," Mrs. Carsen said, stroking Tori's blond hair. "Of course you're scared. If you weren't scared, you'd be a robot, not my baby."

"But what if I can't skate? What if I can't even finish my routine?"

Mrs. Carsen held Tori away from her and dabbed at her daughter's eyes with a tissue.

"Tori," she said firmly, "you don't have to finish your routine. You just have to do the best you can."

Tori glanced at Dan. He nodded.

"That's all you can ask of yourself, champ," he said. "Just go out there and try your hardest. Don't worry about what's going to happen after that."

He grinned and gave her a thumbs-up sign.

She walked down the long hall toward the rink. She heard the announcer call her name.

She stepped onto the ice.

A hush fell over the arena as she skated to center ice and took her opening pose.

How many of them saw the *Time* article? Tori wondered. How many of them are waiting for me to collapse?

As the first notes of her music played, Tori felt frozen in place. Panic flowed through her body. Move! she screamed to herself.

Then she was skating across the ice. She moved into her opening sequence of spins. She began the powerful back crossovers that led to a double axel. Then a serpentine pattern of steps took her into a triple Lutz.

She was listening to her music so intently that she barely heard the applause from the audience. Suddenly she felt as if the music were inside her. The familiar notes from the opera *Faust* were touching and beautiful.

She felt a sense of peace come over her.

And she felt the joy of skating fill her.

Everything was coming together. It was the first time in a month that she hadn't felt scared while she skated. She didn't care anymore if she fell or made a fool of herself. She just wanted to skate as hard and as well as she could.

It was time for her triple-triple combination jump.

There had originally been two triple-triple jumps in her program. She would have been the first woman to perform two triple-triples in competition if she had pulled them off.

But Dan had taken out the second triple-triple combination—even before he knew Tori was sick. He could tell there was something wrong with her and that she didn't have enough energy for the second triple jump combination.

She knew that meant she had to nail the only triple-triple jump in her program. She saw in her mind exactly how the triple toe loop–triple toe loop was supposed to look.

She did it, exactly as she had imagined it. The crowd roared.

Tori relaxed her body for a millisecond, enjoying the feeling of the ice beneath her and of her body rushing through space. She felt as if she were at the center of the universe as she began her combination spin, starting with a camel, then moving into a layback. She arched her back strongly and stretched her arms above her until she could see the ice. She moved into a back sit–sit spin and glided out backward.

The music slowed. She skated around the rink, feeling the sad and serious music in her bones. She wove through outside-inside-outside edge changes. She leaped into a triple salchow with a Mohawk, then stretched into another layback spin.

A few more pretty moves, and then it was time for her triple loop jump. The one that had originally been a triple loop–triple loop.

Split seconds before Tori took off, she knew what she was going to do. She was going for the second triple-triple!

She leaped up with all her strength. She landed the first jump perfectly and launched into the second without pausing. She spun through the air. For a second she felt as if time had stopped. Then she landed solidly. Perfectly.

The packed arena went wild. People stood up and screamed and cheered and stamped their feet. She had performed two triple-triple jump combinations in one program. Tori had just made skating history! The audience was going wild.

But Tori didn't hear a sound.

She was alone with her skates on the rink. Her moves were perfect, but there was more to it than that. All the emotions of the previous days came through in the raw power of her movement. There was frustration, fear, and triumph in every stroke of her blades. She didn't just land jumps. She owned them. A difficult leap was as natural to her as breathing.

The audience could feel Tori's emotions pouring from her fingertips as she performed her routine. And Tori could feel their support. She skated for them, for Dan, for her friends, for her mother. Most of all, she skated for herself. She skated for the love of skating.

Near the end of the routine, the music became fast again. She curved into forward crossovers, a forward inside rocker, a back crossover, back inside three. Then she straightened out for her triple flip. All of a sudden, she could practically feel the audience's support holding her up. The music reached a crashing crescendo, the intricate moves of her straight-line footwork reached a furious pace. Finally she sped into a split jump, then into a stag leap, and ended with a death drop.

As Tori stood, tears streamed from her eyes. Her arms were stretched wide, and the bright lights made it impossible to see anything. Her chest heaved with exhaustion and emotion. She knew in her soul that she had skated her best. And the audience's applause confirmed her feelings.

She held that feeling for a long moment. Then she skated to the boards and joined Dan and her mother. The three of them walked to the velvet-draped bench in front of the television cameras.

Young skaters picked up the bouquets and stuffed animals that had been tossed onto the ice and brought them over to her, shyly dropping them in her lap. She accepted them gracefully, handing some to Mrs. Carsen.

"You skated like . . . I didn't know you could skate so perfectly," Mrs. Carsen murmured, holding Tori tightly.

Tori tried to catch her breath. Her chest was heaving. Dan patted her face with a towel.

Tori's body was buzzing with energy, and her heart felt as if it would burst. She had been competing since she was a child. But competing had never felt like this. She wanted to close her eyes and hold on to the movements she had just made on the ice. She felt triumphant and full of life.

Finally the scores came up. As the numbers were

read aloud, the announcer's voice booming through the arena, Tori strained to see them. First there were the technical merit scores. She heard an excited cheer burst from her mouth as they all floated between 5.7 and 5.9. The next moments crawled by as she waited for the presentation scores.

Wild cheering drowned out the announcer's voice. Tori leaned way over to see the numbers, then whipped back to meet her mother's eyes. Her breath seemed to leave her body. Her scores were all high and included two sixes.

"I'm so proud," Mrs. Carsen said.

"I can't believe it!" Tori finally squeaked out.

She looked directly into the television cameras and gave a proud, winning smile.

"With your short program scores, that puts you in third place overall, right behind Amber and Tracy Wilkins," Dan informed her, folding her into a tight hug. "Do you know what that means?"

"I think so," Tori said. She was trembling, and tears filled her eyes again. She knew exactly what that meant. She had done it. She was going to the Olympics!

"How about Jill?" she asked Dan.

"Well, as I said, Amber won, and Tracy Wilkins came in second. You're third. Fiona Bartlet came in fourth. Jill came in fifth. And Carla," Dan added, "well, Carla fell three times."

Tori stood and waved at the cameras, then stepped a few paces over so that she could see the scores again.

The numbers wavered crazily. She dashed the tears away from her eyes. She had to get a clear picture. This was what she had always worked for! But the scores were darkening. Orange fireworks seemed to burst at the edges of her vision. A rushing sound filled her head.

Suddenly the strength that she had felt during her program left her. Her knees buckled, and she pitched forward helplessly. She collapsed into her mother's arms.

Tori stared at the ceiling of the arena. She fought to stay conscious.

She had just given a medal-winning performance— the best of her life. Her shot at the Olympics was finally here. And now her body was betraying her again.

She looked at her mother's face. Mrs. Carsen was deathly white as she leaned over her, gripping her tightly.

"Mom," Tori whispered. "Mom."

Everything went black.

TO BE CONCLUDED IN
GOLD MEDAL DREAMS #3,
CHANCE OF A LIFETIME!

Don't miss *Chance of a Lifetime*, the exciting conclusion of the Gold Medal Dreams miniseries!

CHANCE OF A LIFETIME

Tori's dream is coming true—she's going to the Olympic Games! But Tori is scared. Very scared. She has a disease that is draining her strength. She needed every ounce of her courage and energy just to qualify for the Olympics. Now even walking can be torture. But Tori must skate in front of the world. If she fails, she'll let down everyone she loves—and her entire country.

Tori knows this may be her only chance . . .

The chance of a lifetime.

Turn the page to read an exciting chapter from Chance of a Lifetime, *on sale at your local bookstore next month!*

"**Y**ou looked much better today," Dan Trapp said as Tori stepped off the ice a few hours later.

"I *felt* much better," Tori said. She wiped the beads of sweat off her forehead with a towel. In fact, she had felt great out there. She'd landed every jump cleanly. She could have skated for at least another hour.

Tori didn't tell Dan *why* she had skated so well. Every time she pictured her father's face, she felt a surge of anger. And it seemed as if the anger made her stronger.

"I have to admit, I was concerned yesterday," Dan said. "You didn't have a very good practice. But you put all my fears to rest today." Dan squeezed Tori's shoulders. "The moment's almost here. I'm so proud of you."

"Thanks," Tori said. She leaned against Dan. She'd never had a coach she liked working with so much— or a coach who had more faith in her.

"You know what to do this afternoon," Dan said.

"Rest. Stretch. Take a hot bath. And visualize your program. Your perfect, *winning* program."

Tori nodded. "Okay." She turned to head for the locker room and nearly crashed into Natalia. "Hey! You made it after all." Tori laughed, feeling exhilarated after her practice. "So," she added, remembering Natalia's problem, "did you talk to Jelena?"

"She wasn't there. You know how I was saying that she has a bunch of weird traditions? Well, she gets superstitious about seeing the ice she's going to compete on the day before the competition," Natalia explained.

"So how's she going to practice?" Tori asked, glancing at the clock on the wall. "I thought the Russian team was coming in at noon."

"Everyone else is, but not Jelena. To focus, she always goes somewhere else, where nobody knows her and there are no judges or coaches around. She skates by herself," Natalia said. "When I went to her room, she was already gone. Papa told me she probably went off to the public rink. I am going to find her there. I came by to see if you want to go."

"To the public rink in Nagano? Now?" Tori pulled a heavy sweatshirt over her skating dress. "I don't know. I should go back to our room and lie down for a while. I had a great practice, and I don't want to jinx it by skating any more today."

"Oh." Natalia's face fell. "Are you sure? Afterward we could all have hot chocolate or hot sushi or whatever they drink here. Wait—not sushi—sake! No, wait—sake is wine. We're definitely not having that. But could you come? You don't have to skate."

Tori hesitated. "Maybe . . . I don't know."

"Tori, I know you need to take it easy," Natalia said. "But it would be a big help to me if you came along. I am so awkward talking to Jelena lately." She scuffed the floorboard with her sneaker.

Tori could see that Natalia was still struggling to find a way to talk to her sister. "I can't promise anything right now," Tori said. "But if I feel better after I take a nap, I'll come meet you. Okay?"

"Thanks. That's good enough for me," Natalia said with a grin. "Papa said Jelena would be at the public rink for a couple of hours. Come down after you have rested—please?" She clasped her hands together.

"I'll try," Tori promised. "Now I'd better get back to the hotel before my mother launches a search party!"

～ ～

Tori unwrapped the towel from her head and started to brush her long blond hair. She must have soaked in the big hotel bathtub for an hour, lying still and doing Dan's visualization exercises. She felt calm and relaxed.

If only the short program were tonight, instead of tomorrow night. The way her health had been lately, she never knew how she would feel from one day to the next. She didn't want to take a chance by waiting.

She sat down on her bed and turned on the television, flipping to the Olympic Coverage Channel. The station broadcast Olympic news all day long, in English. While she got dressed, she listened to a story about snowboarding making its debut as an Olympic sport. The story ended. An anchor came on to give a recap of the day's top stories. Tori scooped up her tiny pearl earrings from the bedside table and put them on as she watched.

"And now, a very special, exclusive interview. One of the most touching stories to come from the Nagano Olympics is that of Tori Carsen. This promising young figure skater's seemingly endless future of medals has been cut short. She received a diagnosis of myotonic muscular dystrophy just a month before the Olympics."

Tori dropped an earring onto the carpet. Why were they doing a story all about her? And why did they have to focus on her illness?

"Our reporter spoke to Tori's father this morning," the anchor continued as Tori leaned over to pick up her earring. "And here is that interview with James Carsen, in its entirety."

Tori sat bolt upright, knocking her head against the bed frame. What? Her father was giving an exclusive interview about her? He barely knew her!

The TV image switched from the anchor's desk to the snow-covered ice arena, the White Ring. "A daughter is precious," a reporter's voice said as sappy music played. "And even more precious is the daughter whom the father never got a chance to know . . . until now."

Tori stared at the television, stunned. The picture shifted to the reporter, standing next to her father outside the arena. Tori felt as if she were going to burst from anger. Since when did he have the right to talk about her as if he knew her?

"According to James Carsen, Tori's chances of winning an Olympic medal grow dimmer with each day that passes. Tori is suffering from the horrible disease of muscular dystrophy."

"Shut up!" Tori screamed at the screen. "It's not like that!" She did have a chance to medal—Dan said so, Natalia said so, everyone said so. How dare her father tell a reporter otherwise?

"What brought you to Nagano?" the reporter asked, holding the microphone toward Mr. Carsen. "After all these years of separation, what made you decide to contact your daughter now?"

"I had to see Tori. I wanted to see her skate, but I also needed to talk to her about the muscular dystrophy. It's a genetically inherited disease. My mother passed it on to me, and I passed it on to Tori. I have such a mild case, I didn't think about it when my wife and I had Tori."

"That's the truth," Tori seethed, glaring at him. "Because you never think about anything but yourself!"

"How *is* Tori?" the reporter asked. "Should we be rooting for her to win the gold . . . or rooting for her health?"

"Her health seems pretty good. But she's weaker than I expected," Mr. Carsen said. "Sometimes this disease strikes fast. In Tori's case it seems to be doing that. I'm afraid her skating career may come to an end sooner than she thinks."

"You don't know anything!" Tori cried. She clicked the remote, shutting off the TV. She couldn't take any more. She had to get out of the hotel suite. She needed some fresh air.

Tori strode through the living room to her mother and Roger's bedroom. She was about to open the door and ask if anyone wanted to go for a walk when she heard them talking.

"I can't believe he'd do an interview like that," her mother was saying. "They must have paid him. I wouldn't put it past him to take money for talking about his child."

"I can't believe he thinks that *this* is the way to get involved in Tori's life," Roger said.

"That's just it—that's what I've been trying to tell Tori. He *doesn't* think!" Mrs. Carsen said. "Now he's totally disrupting Tori's life. She's too fragile, Roger. She can't handle all the stress of the Olympics as it is!"

Tori turned away from the door. She couldn't handle all the stress? Was that what her mother thought? She'd been handling more stress than anyone could possibly imagine. And now not even her mother believed in her!

It was true that sometimes Tori felt fragile and weak. But she could still skate! She'd had a fantastic practice today. Now everyone thought she was going to collapse onto the ice.

I'm not going to crumple, Tori told herself. I won't let them all be right.

She grabbed her skate bag and a jacket and walked out the door, closing it quietly behind her. All she needed was a little extra practice time with Jelena. She'd show everyone how fragile she was—by winning a medal!

America's Top Pairs Skaters

Meet three couples who hope to win gold at the 1998 Winter Games–if they qualify!

It takes endless patience and trust to skate a pairs program. If one partner fails, they both fail. But when they perform a difficult program in perfect unison, the results are magic!

Jenni Meno and Todd Sand

Paul Harvath

This red-haired couple shares an Olympic love story. And Jenni and Todd could be one of the United States' best hopes for an Olympic medal in 1998.

They placed second at the 1997 Nationals and fifth

at the 1997 World Championships. Both times they finished just behind another talented U.S. team, Kyoko Ina and Jason Dungjen—a pair they've beaten for the national title in the past.

If Jenni and Todd look as if they're in love when they skate, it's because they are! They met at the 1992 Olympics, each skating with a different partner. They began dating and soon started skating together as well. They became engaged at the 1994 Olympics, where they skated together for a fifth-place finish. The couple was married in July 1995 in Jenni's hometown, Westlake, Ohio.

Jenni started skating when she was eight. Todd started skating when he was ten.

Todd and Jenni list another skating couple, the late Sergei Grinkov and his widow, Ekaterina Gordeeva, as the athletes they admire most. Why? Because Ekaterina and Sergei demonstrated exactly what pairs skating should be: two partners skating in perfect unity, expressing one emotion.

Stats:

Jenni was born November 19, 1970, in Pompton Plains, New Jersey.
She is five feet tall and weighs ninety-six pounds.
Todd was born October 30, 1963, in Burbank, California.
He is five feet, eleven inches tall and weighs 165 pounds.
Training town: Lake Arrowhead, California.

Kyoko Ina and Jason Dungjen

Paul Harvath

This couple always gives Jenni Meno and Todd Sand a run for their money. Kyoko and Jason's skating is improving faster than the speed of light.

At only five feet tall and ninety-two pounds, Kyoko is a tiny powerhouse. She stands a foot shorter than her partner.

Judges look for a special spark between partners, and that's what Kyoko and Jason try to show them. They must be doing it right, because they won the Nationals in 1997 and went on to place fourth at the 1997 World Championships.

Kyoko was only four when her parents brought her to New York City to see the huge Christmas tree that towers over the skating rink at Rockefeller Center. Kyoko liked the tree—but she loved the skaters! She started skating soon after that. Jason started skating when he was eleven.

Stats:

Kyoko was born October 11, 1972, in Tokyo.
She is five feet tall and weighs ninety-two pounds.
Jason was born September 27, 1967, in Detroit.
He is six feet tall and weighs 170 pounds.
Training town: Monsey, New York.

Shelby Lyons and Brian Wells

Paul Harvath

Brian Wells went on a cross-country search to find his perfect partner. He found her in a pixie named Shelby Lyons. Shelby, a pretty brunette, is less than five feet tall!

The young pair placed an incredible tenth at the 1996 Worlds, after skating together for only two years.

They finished third at the Nationals in 1996 and fourth in 1997.

Shelby started skating when she was four. She also competes as a singles skater and was the junior ladies singles champion at the 1996 Nationals. Her goal is to someday make the U.S. Olympic Team in singles *and* pairs.

Brian is one of nine children. He started skating when he was eleven. His first partner was his sister, Ann-Marie, who eventually lost interest in skating.

Stats:

Shelby was born May 24, 1981, in Oswego, New York.
She is four feet, ten inches tall and weighs seventy pounds.
Brian was born September 23, 1970, in Carmel, California.
He is five feet, five inches tall and weighs 135 pounds.
Training town: Colorado Springs.

Ice Dancers

Beauty, elegance, and sparkle—that's what these couples demonstrate when they glide through their programs. Meet three of America's top ice dancing teams.

Kate Robinson and Peter Breen

Michelle Harvath

These lanky partners make a striking pair. Their long legs seem to slink across the ice, and their elegance, skill, and creativity earned them the bronze medal at the 1997 U.S. Championships. They hope to dance their way to a spot on the Olympic team after two fourth-place finishes at the U.S. Championships.

Kate started skating at nine. She enjoys cooking, reading, and artwork. She also loves writing. She hopes to be a published writer someday.

Peter graduated from Boston University in 1993 with a degree in health sciences. Soon after, he was able to put his education to good use: In 1994 he performed CPR on a Danish cyclist who had a heart attack at the Olympic Training Center. Peter received a Meritorious Action Award from the United States' Olympic Committee for saving the cyclist's life.

Peter began skating at age seven and is now a certified athletic trainer.

Stats:

Kate was born December 8, 1978, in Peoria, Illinois.
She is five feet, six inches tall and weighs 108 pounds.
Peter was born October 29, 1969, in Brockton,
Massachusetts.
He is six feet, one inch tall and weighs 175 pounds.
Training town: Bloomfield Hills, Michigan.

Elizabeth Punsalan
and Jerod Swallow

Paul Harvath

This well-matched pair looks like the perfect couple—and they are! They began skating together in 1989 and were married in 1993 after a yearlong engagement. They have become very strong contenders for an Olympic medal.

Elizabeth and Jerod are known for their dramatic

on-ice personalities. Their fourth Nationals win in 1997 was as solid as their footwork.

In 1994, they made the Olympic team—only to finish a disappointing fifteenth. But these three-time U.S. Champions hope to place higher at the 1998 Olympics. Their hard work and creativity should make them tough to beat.

Elizabeth began skating at seven. Like many athletes, she's superstitious—she *always* ties her right skate first.

Jerod started skating when he was ten.

Stats:

Elizabeth was born January 9, 1971, in Syracuse, New York.

She is five feet, five inches tall and weighs 111 pounds.

Jerod was born October 18, 1968, in Ann Arbor, Michigan.

He is five feet, nine inches tall and weighs 145 pounds.

Training town: Bloomfield Hills, Michigan.

Eve Chalom and Mathew Gates

Paul Harvath

These two are often playful in their programs—and always technically strong. They just keep getting better and better! The couple came in third at the 1996 U.S. National Championships. They climbed to second at the 1997 Nationals. Eve started skating at nine and has never let any obstacle stop her from doing

11

what she loves. She was born almost deaf and has since lost most of the hearing in both ears. She uses a hearing aid to hear her skating music.

Mathew began skating at thirteen. He was born in England and came to the United States five years ago. Because he still has not received his final U.S. citizenship papers, the pair will not be able to compete in the 1998 U.S. Olympics. But that's not going to stop them from working hard and getting ready for the next competition.

Eve enjoys reading and writing poetry. She also likes to play with her cat and two pet ferrets. Mathew's interests include art, music, pool, and table tennis.

Stats:

Eve was born October 22, 1979, in Detroit.
She is five feet, one inch tall and weighs ninety-six pounds.
Mathew was born June 29, 1975, in Hitchin, England.
He is five feet, six inches tall and weighs 130 pounds.
Training town: Bloomfield Hills, Michigan.

LEARN TO SKATE!

SKATE WITH U.S.
A SPECIAL PROGRAM FOR BEGINNERS

WHAT IS **SKATE WITH U.S.**?

Designed by the United States Figure Skating Association (USFSA) and sponsored by the United States Postal Service, Skate With U.S. is a beginning ice-skating program that is fun, challenging, and rewarding. Skaters of all ages are welcome!

HOW DO I JOIN **SKATE WITH U.S.**?

Skate With U.S. is offered at many rinks and clubs across the country. Contact your local rink or club to see if it offers the USFSA Basic Skills program. Or **call 1-800-269-0166** for more information about the Skate With U.S. program in your area.

WHAT DO I GET WHEN I JOIN **SKATE WITH U.S.**?

When you join Skate With U.S. through a club or a rink, you will be registered as an official USFSA Basic Skills Member, and you will receive:

- Official Basic Skills Membership Card
- Basic Skills Record Book with stickers
- Official Basic Skills member patch
- Year patch, denoting membership year
  And much, much more!

PLUS you may be eligible to participate in a "Compete With U.S." competition hosted by sponsoring clubs and rinks!

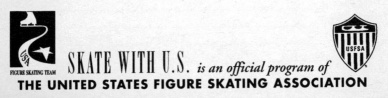

SKATE WITH U.S. *is an official program of*
THE UNITED STATES FIGURE SKATING ASSOCIATION

A FAN CLUB—JUST FOR YOU!

JOIN THE USA FIGURE SKATING INSIDE TICKET FAN CLUB!

As a member of this special skating fan club, you get:

- **Six issues of SKATING MAGAZINE!**
  For the inside edge on what's happening on and off the ice!

- **Your very own copy of MAGIC MEMORIES ON ICE!**
  A 90-minute video produced by ABC Sports featuring the world's greatest skaters!

- **An Official USA FIGURE SKATING TEAM Pin!**
  Available only to Inside Ticket Fan Club members!

- **A limited-edition photo of the U.S. World Figure Skating Team!**
  Available only to Inside Ticket Fan Club members!

- **The Official USA FIGURE SKATING INSIDE TICKET Membership Card!** For special discounts on USA Figure Skating collectibles and memorabilia!

To join the USA FIGURE SKATING INSIDE TICKET Fan Club, fill out the form below and send it with $24.95, plus $3.95 for shipping and handling (U.S. funds only, please!), to:

> Sports Fan Network
> USA Figure Skating Inside Ticket
> P.O. Box 581
> Portland, Oregon 97207-0581

Or call the Sports Fan Network membership hotline at **1-800-363-8796!**

NAME:_____

ADDRESS:_____

CITY:_____**STATE:**_____**ZIP:**_____

PHONE: (____)_____**DATE OF BIRTH:**_____